Run for Cover

The Story of the Gene Machine

To Fran, for her patience and support

Run for Cover

The Story of the Gene Machine

TOM MCCAUGHREN

WOLFHOUND PRESS
Celebrating 25 *Years*

First published in 1999 by
Wolfhound Press Ltd
68 Mountjoy Square
Dublin 1, Ireland
Tel: (353-1) 874 0354
Fax: (353-1) 872 0207

The Arts Council
An Chomhairle Ealaíon

Wolfhound Press receives financial assistance from The Arts Council/An Chomhairle Ealaíon, Dublin, Ireland.

British Library Cataloguing in Publication Data
A catalogue record for this book is available from the British Library.

ISBN 0-86327-779-9

10 9 8 7 6 5 4 3 2 1

Cover Illustration: Aileen Caffrey
Cover Design: Slick Fish Design, Dublin
Text Illustrations: Jeanette Dunne
Typesetting: Wolfhound Press
Printed and bound by MPG Books Ltd., Bodmin, Cornwall

CONTENTS

1

A Plague of Frogs

Listen to the wind. Listen to the wind, for it caresses
Mother Earth and tells you all you need to hear ....
Caress the wind. Caress the wind, for it listens to
Mother Earth and shows you all you need to see ....

For many creatures of the wild, the wind is the high-
way of life. Whatever the season, it carries the scents
and sounds of nature, and a whole lot more. And so the
words of wisdom of the great god Vulpes came to the
mind of the fox on the hill, as he cocked his ear to the
summer breeze and caressed it with his fine, pointed
nose. 'Listen to the wind. Listen to the wind,' the fox
god had decreed, and so he did.

The fox on the hill would not have been aware that man had also listened to the wind and, in one of his more poetic moments, had written:

What way does the Wind come? What way does he go?
He rides over the water, and over the snow,
Through wood, and through vale; and o'er rocky height,
Which the goat cannot climb, takes his sounding flight;
He tosses about in every bare tree,
As, if you look up, you plainly may see ....

However, the fox on the hill had been taught to ask the very same questions about the wind. Which way did it come? Which way did it go? As a cub, he had been taught to regard the wind as a friend. Having ascertained which way it had come, he would read it just as he would read the signs of nature as he passed through the fields. If it warned of danger, he would simply go along with it, knowing that it would carry his scent away from those who sought to harm him. Otherwise, he would sit and enjoy it. For its scents and its sounds painted a picture of his surroundings. As he drew them in through his nostrils, he could see, in his mind's eye, what man would call 'a map' of the hills and fields, the streams and rivers, the flowers and the trees.

Unlike man, whose senses are not as developed, the fox could hear the wind rushing through a distant gap between two hills, then slowing down to caress the new grass in the meadows. He could hear it rustling the leaves of the hazels that covered the hill beyond the river. He could hear it singing as it squeezed between the slender needles of the swaying pines. He could hear it whispering sweet nothings as it brushed aside the broad leaves of the chestnut and sycamore. He could hear it whistling softly as it pursed its lips to avoid the toothed leaves of the mighty oak. And he could scent many of the creatures over which it passed: the birds in the trees, the mice in the hedgerows, the herons in the river, the rabbits on the hill.

Hop-along sniffed the wind again. The scent of the rabbits was usually the strongest, simply because there were more of them. But not today. And, not for the first time, he wondered why. He had been hoping to catch one unawares, and as hunger gnawed at his insides, he cursed the trapper whose steel-jawed trap had robbed him of one of his paws.

Crossing the river, Hop-along came across paw-prints in the mud. For some strange reason, he couldn't make up his mind whether they had been left by a fox or a cat. Probably both, he concluded. Perhaps a fox following a cat, or a cat following a fox. Confused, he kept going, hobbling in and out of the Hill of Hazels. Here and there he found rabbit burrows beneath the bushes. Fresh droppings in the vicinity told him that the burrows were occupied, but there was no sign of the rabbits. Once, as he sniffed the droppings, he became aware that he was being watched and, looking up, saw a long-tailed field mouse peering down at him, its large ears listening to his every move.

The mouse was sitting on the branch of a hawthorn bush, washing its whiskers with its front paws. Had man been looking at it, he would have thought that it was a fearless little creature, casually grooming itself in the face of danger, but Hop-along knew better. Sometimes, a field mouse would clean its whiskers after feeding. Holding its dampened forepaws close to its face, it would draw them downwards over its whiskers. At other times, however, it would go through the ritual out of sheer fright, and Hop-along could tell by the way this one nervously twitched its nose that this was one of those times.

Perhaps, thought Hop-along, the field mouse was in such a state of fright that it was too afraid to move. He turned and took a faltering step towards it, but it was a move he made by instinct rather than from any realistic hope that he might be able to catch it. The mouse immediately turned and, with a squeak, took a flying leap onto a nearby briar, from which it quickly scurried to safety. The squeak was so high-pitched that man would not have heard it, but it was audible to the fox, and to any other predator that might be in the vicinity. It was also obvious to Hop-along that it was not a warning squeak, intended to alert the mouse's family to danger. It was a squeak that was born of fear, and once again he found himself wondering what had given the mouse such a fright. Hardly a three-legged fox.

Making his way along the river, Hop-along paused to watched a long-legged heron take to the air and fly ponderously over the meadows. A good hunter, he thought. Patient in its wait for fish, deadly accurate in picking them out of the water. Hobbling on, he climbed up onto a grassy knoll. There, a fallen tree was slowly being reclaimed by the earth, through a process of decay and decimation. Prising off a loose piece of bark, he found various creepy-crawlies underneath — copper-coloured centipedes, black-backed beetles and juicy white larvae. Having devoured these with relish, he lay down on his side and, using his remaining front paw, scooped out a number of slugs which were sleeping in a slimy world of their own in the grass beneath the trunk.

Such food was a poor substitute for a rabbit, and Hop-along was still hungry. He nibbled at a cluster of small brown toadstools, and when they had been consumed he turned his attention to a fungus that had taken root in the decaying remains of the fallen tree. Not as nice as mushrooms, he told himself, but at least it was edible, and he gulped it down in a desperate effort to appease his hunger.

Once again, Hop-along caressed the wind with his nose and savoured the scents of Mother Earth. Once again he wondered where the rabbits had gone. His thoughts returned to the field mouse, and he wondered what had given it such a fright. Whatever it was, he reckoned it must have frightened the rabbits too. However, he knew they would have to come out to eat sometime, and he was determined to wait.

It was coming on towards evening now, and Hop-along watched the bright glow of day settle on the hills beyond the woods. Slowly it turned into a ball of fire, and as it dipped behind the hills, it seemed to set the sky alight. Bit by bit the flames spread up through the clouds, until a large part of the sky had turned to red. Somehow, it reminded him of the fire in the fields — of the day when the flames had spread through the corn stubble, singeing the fur of his sick cub, Scab. Those flames had scarred the cub for life, but they had cured him of the itch that had threatened to kill him.

Hop-along looked at the red sky again and wondered if perhaps it was a good omen, a sign of better things to come. He looked at the place where his right paw should have been and thought that he could do with a good omen. A good omen in the form of a good rabbit!

Looking at the flames in the sky again, he found himself thinking of his other cub, Scat. He too had been sick, but a wise old friend — a blind fox called Sage Brush — had nursed him back to health, and now he had settled down in the blackthorns with a lovely little vixen called Flame.

Flame, Flame .... Somehow, Hop-along could think

of nothing but flames. Flames in the sky, flames in his mind .... And then it seemed his whole being was on fire. The flames were spreading up through his mind the same way they had spread through the fields that day long ago, the same way they were now spreading up through the sky. At the same time, the things around him began to change shape, merging from one form to another, like the shadows in a river distorted by the flow of the water.

'Caress the wind,' he heard the great god Vulpes say. 'Caress the wind, for it listens to Mother Earth and shows you all you need to see.'

The voice of Vulpes seemed to come from afar, almost as if it was of another world — the world of the hereafter. To be in that world, however, Hop-along knew he would have to be dead, and he felt very much alive. More alive, in fact, than he had ever felt before. The wind, he could see, was plucking at his fur. Then he felt it reach in under him, and, with the gentleness of a vixen moving a cub, it lifted him up. Next thing he knew, he was being carried across the countryside, like a feather floating on air. And just as the wind allows a feather to kiss the ground now and then, he found himself caressing Mother Earth, then bounding off again to a great height, a height from which he could see all the things a fox ever wanted to see. It was a gentle experience, one so soft and soothing and so all-embracing that he had no fear. Then his paws touched the ground again — all four of them — for he knew without looking that his missing paw had returned. And he was running across the countryside, a kindred spirit of the wind, of Mother Earth, and of all the foxes that had ever lived. But instead of being green, the countryside was blue, and instead of being blue, the sky was the colour of fire. After a while it began to rain, but instead of raining rain, it was raining frogs — and instead of being yellow or green, the frogs were red.

For the first time since he had lost his paw, Hop-along was at one with nature. He was no longer hopping along, no longer hobbling. Instead he was running swiftly on all four legs, a swift and masterful hunter. Mother Earth was a bountiful provider. The frogs were even more numerous than the creepy-crawlies he had found under the bark of the tree. One seemed to fall with every drop of rain, and as it hopped out of the grass towards him, all he had to do was scoop it up in his jaws and swallow it whole.

Strange as it may seem, the frogs still didn't satisfy Hop-along's hunger, and when, at last, he spotted a rabbit running away through the meadow, he immediately gave chase. Unlike all the other rabbits he had seen, it was red, like the frogs, instead of grey. It was also a young rabbit, and, even with his four legs beneath him, he couldn't catch up with it. Twisting and turning, it raced on through the blue grass of the meadows until it came to a bend in the river. There it stopped briefly, to make sure it was far enough ahead, before hopping into a copse of small trees. Some of the trees, Hop-along could see, were bushy, with yellow berries, like those of the rowan tree before they were ripe. Others were pointed and had low, sweeping branches, like the ones he had seen man hang coloured lights on in winter.

There was no sign of man around now, so Hop-along edged his way forward. But before he reached the trees, he heard the rabbit squealing. Cautiously, he made his way in under the branches.

There, to his astonishment, he saw the rabbit stuck fast in the leaves of a giant daisy. At least, it looked like a daisy, but while the flower at the top was white, the leaves at the bottom were pink and hairy, and at the end of each hair was a blob of water. At least, it looked like a blob of water — but, as the rabbit had discovered to its cost, it wasn't water. It was a sticky substance, and it held the rabbit so firmly that it could hardly move. When it did try to move, more hairs bent over and helped to hold it with their blobs.

The rabbit continued to struggle, but eventually the leaf itself bent over. Slowly but surely, the squealing animal was completely enveloped, and he could see it no more.

Mesmerised, Hop-along could only stand and watch. For a while the rabbit continued to struggle inside the sticky leaf. Then it was still, and he knew it was dead. The redness of the rabbit began to seep out through the hairs that had trapped it, and he realised it was being eaten by the plant just as surely as it would have been eaten by a fox.

It was only when Hop-along looked around him that he saw he wasn't in a copse of trees at all, but in a cluster of giant weeds that were almost as tall as man. What he had taken for small fir trees were, in fact, overgrown thistles. Vying for space with the skeletons of last year's giant hogweed, they were thrusting out their long, spear-like leaves as if trying to keep other weeds at arm's length. But, sharp as they were, the spears could not prevent other weeds from taking root, and here and there grew tall stalks of ragwort, whose yellow seed-heads he had mistaken for rowan berries. Nor could the thistles prevent a thick matting of nettles, goosegrass and bindweed from hoisting itself up, and, at its topmost point, large flowers of bindweed looked out triumphantly at the red of the sky. But instead of being white, the trumpets of bindweed were blue, and they nodded across at the flowers on the thistles, which, instead of being blue, were white.

Hop-along now became aware of the pungent smell from the weeds, and as he sniffed around, he also detected the smell of rotten egg. The eggshell, he discovered, was lying nearby. One half was still intact, and, to his astonishment, he could see that the whole egg would have been as big as a turnip. The smell of the weeds and the rotten egg had killed the scent of the rabbit, and, as he looked around in puzzlement, another smell overcame their smell. It was the overpowering smell of fear.

Taking off as fast as he could, Hop-along floated across the countryside again. In no time at all, he found himself standing in a field, looking up at a bird with long legs and short wings. It was even taller than man, and, apart from its long legs, it was the strangest bird he had ever seen, for it had two long necks and two heads, each with the beak of a duck. When he asked it which way he should go, it twisted its long necks around each other, one head saying, 'That way,' the other pointing in the opposite direction and saying, 'That way.' Confused, he was about to ask the strange bird which way it meant, when it uncoiled its necks and he couldn't tell which head had said what.

Wondering which of the bird's heads had been telling him a lie, Hop-along kept going and, a short time later, found himself looking at another bird. This time, it was a rainbow bird, but instead of having a blue head with a delicate fringe on top, it had the head of a rooster, with a massive red comb that wobbled whenever it moved. And its fan-shaped tail, instead of having all the colours of the rainbow, with butterfly eyes to match, had little more colour than the tail of a cock. Hop-along was about to ask this strange bird which way he should go when it crowed, so loudly that he feared it would waken the whole wide world of man. Then, to his astonishment, it wiggled its fan-shaped tail and disappeared.

No sooner had the rainbow bird gone than Hop-along found himself looking up at what he took to be a deer. But when he asked it which way he should go, it raised its long slender neck, pranced nervously with its long slender legs and turned its back on him. However, instead of a back, it had another head, and that head was just as nervous as the one at the other end.

'Which way will I go?' he asked again. Once more the strange animal turned its back — except it wasn't its back, but its other front, and so it kept turning and turning, until he could see it was such a dilly it couldn't make up its mind.

Thinking he would find safety, and perhaps even sanity, down by the river, Hop-along turned tail and sailed over into the meadows. There he found more of the tracks that had puzzled him earlier, and he was wondering if they were the pawprints of a fox or a cat when he became aware that eyes were watching him from a nearby hedge. Looking up, he saw the shadowy outline of a creature that had the long nose of a fox but the short ears of a cat, the long-haired fur of a fox but the sloping tail of a cat, and, overall, the colours of both. But most frightening of all were its eyes, for they were the eyes of a cat.

Once again, Hop-along was beset with fear, and he was glad that he now had four fine paws with which to put a safe distance between himself and this strange land. The problem was, he still didn't know which way to go to get back home.

In another meadow he met a young pig wallowing about in the mud. 'Which way will I go?' he asked it. But the pig, he saw, had two faces. Furthermore, each face seemed to smile and point him in a different direction.

Backing away, he felt a stinging pain in his rear end and, turning, discovered that he had just been attacked by a sheep. However, it wasn't like any other sheep he had seen, for as well as having two horns on its head, it had a long, pointed horn where it should have had a tail. And now, like a wasp defending its nest, it was shunting itself back at great speed, determined, it seemed, to drive this interloper out of its land and into the river.

Hop-along needed no further encouragement. Taking to his heels, he raced across the blue grass of the meadow and flung himself into the river. As he floated away, he head a voice from afar saying, 'Listen to the wind. Listen to the wind.' And he did.

Like a feather drifting on the current, he swirled around and looked at the red of the sky. For a moment he felt as if the wind had reached in under him again and was carrying him across the countryside, caressing Mother Earth as it went. Then the flames in the sky flickered out, all the colours disappeared and everything was black.

2

Fearful Eyes

A lark rose from the meadow and, twittering a song for all to hear, eased itself up into the blue of the sky. Slowly but surely, it rose higher and higher, and the higher it rose, the more it could see. The meadow grass was long and lush and glinted in the morning sun. The flowers of the field were ablaze with colour, and, where they raised their heads above the meadow grass, they nodded and swayed in the summer breeze. On the higher ground, the corn crops were blankets of green, but it was a green into which no other colour was allowed to intrude. It was a greenness that nature had never intended, but which man had engineered.

Little escaped the attention of the lark as it rose and

fell above its nest. It noticed the heron that rose from the river and made its way down towards the lake. It's possible that it may have noticed the inert body of a fox lying on a low mud bank of the river, and may even have wondered how it came to be there. But if it did, it paid no heed and continued to sing, even when it rose so high it was no longer visible from the ground.

Hop-along opened his eyes, then quickly adjusted them to the bright light of day. He saw the space where his right paw should have been and wondered what had happened. He recalled running across the countryside on four fine legs, the wind caressing his fur and his nose caressing the wind. Had it all been a dream? he wondered. Or a nightmare? For now he recalled the strange birds and animals he had met on his travels — the bird with two necks, the deer with two heads, the pig with two faces, the sheep with a horn where it should have had a tail.

Struggling to his feet, Hop-along hobbled up to the meadow. He was hungry, and he looked around for any sign of rabbits. Even a water-rat would do, he thought. To make matters worse, he had a splitting headache and he was thirsty, so he went back down to the river. As he lapped the water, he saw tracks, but he couldn't make out whether they were the pawprints of a fox or a cat.

It was then he remembered the strange creature he had seen on the far side of the river. Combining, as it did, the characteristics of the fox and the cat, it had to be a powerful hunter, and he wondered if it was the reason the rabbits had disappeared. Or was it because of the rabbit-eating daisy?

As he went back over these things in his mind, Hop-along began to wonder if he had imagined some of them. A giant daisy that could eat a rabbit? There was no such thing, he told himself. Then he looked at the strange pawprints again and began to tremble. The pawprints were real, and a three-legged fox, he knew, would have no chance against such an adversary. Turning, he hobbled back up onto the bank and took off, as fast as he could, for home.

How far Hop-along had wandered from the valley where he lived, and how long he had been away, he did not know. All he knew was that he must return to it with all possible speed. According to Old Sage Brush, it was the wind that had formed the valley. The great god Vulpes had caused it to blow so strongly that it had reshaped the mountains to form a place where the fox could survive, and he had called it the Land of Sinna. The wind and the great god Vulpes, Hop-along thought. They had formed the valley, and there, he knew, he would be safe.

Hop-along reckoned that if he followed the river he would find the valley, and when he did, he would make his way up into the blackthorns where She-la, his mate, would be waiting for him. There, too, would be their cub, Scat; his mate, Flame; and their two cubs.

Now and then Hop-along stopped and, with a sense of apprehension he had seldom felt before, looked back over his shoulder. Images of the things he had seen kept going through his mind. The problem was, he didn't know what was real and what was not. He had seen so much on the far side of the river, and yet he had learned so little. Confused and frightened, he contented himself with thoughts of the cubs again and kept going. They were almost weaned now, he told himself, though they still attempted to suckle. When their mother took them out in the evening, they frolicked a lot and played with her tail. Sometimes they became boisterous, but it was only the rough-and-tumble of cubhood. A nip from their mother soon kept them in check.

Hop-along stopped to rest once more and only realised that he had fallen asleep when he felt something nuzzling at his face. Startled, he jumped to his feet and found that it was his mate, She-la.

Both were overjoyed, and they began prancing around each other like cubs. It was a show of emotion which man, if he had seen it, might have mistaken for a ritual of courtship, and it wasn't until Hop-along collapsed that it came to an end. She-la realised immediately that he was exhausted, and so she lay down in the long grass beside him and kept him warm.

As Hop-along slept, She-la groomed him and, in the manner of foxes, spoke softly to him, knowing that even if he didn't understand her it would have a soothing effect on his mind. She assured him that he was back home in the Land of Sinna, told him about the cubs and how big they were getting, and talked to him about his friends — Vickey and Black Tip, Sinnéad and Skulking Dog, and, of course, Old Sage Brush. The old fox, she whispered, had been telling the cubs stories — stories about the time the great god Vulpes had caused a great wind to blow to form the valley for the foxes, and about the times they had left it to go on great journeys. He had told them how they had travelled to the edge of the world and seen the great water, and how, on another occasion, they had strayed into Man's Place and found themselves in the Land of the Giant Ginger Cats.

At the mention of the ginger cats, Hop-along flinched and woke up. He looked around — apprehensively, it seemed to She-la — and told her it was time they were going. She-la looked around too, but she could see nothing that would account for her mate's anxiety. She reckoned he must have been having a bad dream.

From beyond the river, other eyes watched them go. They were the eyes Hop-along had seen in his travels with the wind — eyes that had sent a shiver through his body, for they were those of a creature that was neither a fox nor a cat. And, when the creature turned to go, it left pawprints that belonged to neither one nor the other.

~

Whenever a fox was troubled, it would consult Old Sage Brush. The old fox had taught many of his kind the ways of the wild, and even the older foxes had benefited from his wisdom. Even though he was blind, he had gone on many journeys with them and had shown them things that no other foxes had seen. The seasons were weighing heavily on him now, and his body was so light it sometimes seemed that a gust of wind would blow him away. Nevertheless, his mind was as alert as ever, and his wisdom had, if anything, grown with age.

It was to Old Sage Brush, therefore, that She-la turned. She was greatly troubled, not by the fact that Hop-along had been away so long and had returned in such a pitiful state, but by the change that had come over him. *Learn to listen and listen to learn*, the old fox had told them, and when her mate refused to tell her what had happened to him, she tended him with great patience and forbearance and she listened. And it was what she heard him tell the cubs that troubled her even more.

'You mustn't cross the river,' she overheard him

warn the cubs. 'Whatever you do, you must stay on this side.'

'But why?' asked Blaze.

'Because there are great dangers over there,' he told them.

'What kind of dangers?' asked Firefly.

Hop-along leaned a little closer to them, saying, 'There are birds over there that are as tall as man, and they've two necks and two beaks. And there are deer with two heads, pigs with two faces and sheep with horns at both ends.' The cubs laughed, but he went on, 'I'm not joking. I've seen them. There are also plants that can eat rabbits — fox cubs too, if you're not careful!'

The cubs were no longer laughing, and She-la was tempted to intervene, as she didn't want them to have nightmares. But she held back and listened.

'What's more,' Hop-along continued, 'it's the territory of another hunter.'

'You mean another fox?' asked Firefly.

'Not a fox,' said Hop-along.

'A cat?' asked Blaze.

Hop-along shook his head. 'Not a cat. Well, maybe it is, but it's neither one nor the other, and it's very dangerous.'

'You mean, it's half-fox and half-cat?' asked Blaze.

Hop-along nodded gravely.

'But we've been told there's no such thing,' protested Firefly.

'Oh, but there is,' Hop-along assured them. 'I've seen it. It's got the nose of a fox, but I've looked into its eyes, and they're the eyes of a cat. So do what I tell you and don't cross the river.'

Later, when She-la challenged Hop-along about what she had heard, he shrugged and said it was just a story he had told the cubs to keep them from wandering too far from the earth. She-la, however, wasn't convinced. He had been in a dreadful state when she had found him at the river, he wasn't sleeping well, and he had become very moody. She was beginning to wonder if it was because of what had happened to him on the other side of the river, and then she had heard him telling this story about the strange creatures that were to be found there .... Perhaps, she thought, it was time to consult Old Sage Brush.

Since his return, Hop-along had stayed close to the blackthorns, and it was also clear to the cubs' mother, Flame, that he was moping about something.

'Old Sage Brush has promised to take the cubs out hunting,' she told him. When there was no response, she smiled and added, 'Hunting titmice. Why don't you come? It'll be a bit of a laugh.' However, it was obvious that Hop-along wasn't in a mood for laughing, so she left him to his thoughts.

To Flame's surprise, She-la volunteered to go with her, and, as they led the cubs up through the woods towards the oak tree where the old fox lived, they left Hop-along and his worries behind them.

'Tell me again,' said Flame. 'What did Old Sage Brush say you were going to hunt?'

'Titmice,' replied Blaze.

'Have you ever seen a titmouse?' asked She-la.

Both cubs shook their heads, and Firefly said, 'Just the mice that live in the blackthorns. And they're not titmice, are they?'

She-la smiled and shook her head. 'Titmice have longer tails.'

'Longer than the long-tailed field mouse?' asked Firefly.

'Much longer,' said Flame, 'and they're much harder to catch!'

'But you should consider yourselves very lucky,' added She-la. 'The old fox is a great teacher.'

The lesson the cubs were about to receive wasn't their first one. As soon as they had been old enough, Flame had taken them out of the blackthorns each evening and, with Scat's help, had started the long process of showing them how to fend for themselves. How to locate a worm, for example, and then pull it out of the ground with just the right amount of tension to overcome its resistance but without breaking it. It looked easy, but at first the cubs always broke the worm. They had to be shown how to test the tension of the pulling action with their paws, even massage a stubborn worm with a paw until it lost its grip in the ground. Once they had mastered that technique, they had learned their first lesson.

Mousing was the next thing the cubs had learned, and it involved using their ears, which by that stage had become long and black and much more foxlike. First they had to rotate their ears to pinpoint a mouse from the rustle it made in the undergrowth. Then they had to take what their parents called 'the mouse-leap'. This was a long leap during which they steered themselves in the air, with their tails, in such a way that they landed with their forepaws on their quarry. It was tricky, especially the bit where they had to steer themselves with their tails, but eventually they got the hang of it. And now they had progressed to the next stage — a lesson with Old Sage Brush.

When they arrived at the oak tree where the old fox had his earth, She-la asked Flame to go on ahead with the cubs. Sensing that she wanted to talk to the old fox on her own, Flame obliged.

'What troubles you?' asked Old Sage Brush, as they walked along beneath the trees.

She-la smiled and wondered how the old fox could sense that something was bothering her. 'It's Hop-along,' she told him. 'He's been acting very strange.'

'In what way?'

'It started after I found him on the river-bank. He was in a dreadful state, and it took a lot of effort to nurse him back to health. Physically, I suppose, he's fine, but he's not the same. There's something on his mind. He won't talk to me about it — and now he's started telling the cubs strange stories about things he saw on the other side of the river.'

'What kind of things?'

'Things with two heads. Birds as tall as man. Plants that eat rabbits. And a creature that is half-fox, half-cat.'

The old fox stopped. 'The fox can't mate with the cat. There's no such thing.'

'I know, but he told the cubs he had looked into its eyes and they were the eyes of a cat.' She-la paused. 'He says he's just trying to frighten them so that they won't cross the river and wander too far away. But I don't know .... Somehow, I get a feeling there's more to it than that. He just hasn't been the same since he came back.'

Hearing the excited voices of the cubs ahead of them, they walked on again.

'Remember the time we strayed into Man's Place?' asked Old Sage Brush. 'And we found ourselves in the Land of the Giant Ginger Cats?'

'Of course I do,' said She-la.

'I couldn't see them, of course,' the old fox continued. 'But you and your friends told me of the strange creatures you saw there. Animals with necks so long they could eat from the trees. Others with noses so long they could eat off the ground without even bending. And, of course, the giant ginger cats!'

'But that was Man's Place,' said She-la, 'and he was keeping those animals in cages. This is different. We're only talking about the far side of the river. And I mean, it's not natural — plants that eat rabbits, birds with two heads, an animal that is half-cat, half-fox.'

'Perhaps it's just his imagination,' suggested Old Sage Brush. 'Another story to keep the cubs occupied and, as he says, to keep them from wandering too far from the earth.'

'But he says he's looked into the eyes of this creature,' She-la reminded him. 'And that they're the eyes of a cat. He's frightened. I know him. And he's afraid of what will happen to the cubs if they go there. I'm sure of it.'

'To the fearful eye, all is threatening,' observed the old fox. 'And Hop-along has more reason to fear than most foxes.'

She-la sighed. 'I know, but still, I wonder.'

'Well, don't,' said Old Sage Brush. 'We'll keep an eye on him. And, if necessary, we will go across the river ourselves to see what is to be seen.'

She-la smiled, and felt comforted. She knew from experience that, even though he was blind, the old fox could often see in a way in which a fully sighted fox could not. And now, as the cubs frisked around him and implored him to show them how to hunt the titmouse, he was about to demonstrate this once again.

Most birds, it seemed, had already mated and laid their eggs. Blue tits were especially busy, creeping in and around the branches of the trees in their search for food. Oblivious to the foxes who watched from below, they twisted and turned, flashing their yellow underparts and giving the trees a splash of colour that reflected the primroses in the grass below.

'Your parents have shown you how to use your

teeth and your ears,' Old Sage Brush told the cubs. 'Now you must learn how to use your eyes.'

He stopped. Cocking an ear, he asked them, 'Now, what is that I hear?'

'Long-tailed tits,' replied Blaze. 'Two of them.'

'And what do you notice about them?'

'They've got long tails,' said Firefly.

'Of course,' said the old fox, 'but what else?'

'Their tails are bent,' ventured Blaze.

'Exactly. Now, why do you think that is?'

Perplexed, the cubs waited for him to tell them.

'It's because their tails can't fit into their nest,' Old Sage Brush said.

'Why can't they just hang them over the side?' asked Firefly.

'Because their nest is round,' he explained.

Blaze shrugged. 'What difference does it make, anyway?'

'The point is,' said the old fox, 'when their tails are bent, you know they are nesting, and if they are nesting, then they have eggs.'

'But their eggs must be very small,' said Blaze.

Old Sage Brush nodded. 'That's right. And anyway, their nest is probably in the middle of a thorn-bush.'

'I thought you were going to show us how to hunt the titmouse,' said Firefly, 'not talk about the long-tailed tit.'

The old fox smiled. 'But you *have* been hunting the titmouse. The long-tailed tit, the blue tit — they are all known to us as titmice.' He lay down, and the others lay down around him. Still addressing the cubs, he continued, 'Hunting, you will find, takes a lot of cunning and effort. And, of course, it is not without its dangers. By observing the titmouse, you will have learned two things. One is that very small things are

important, as they may tell you a lot. Even the tail of
the titmouse will tell you that the nesting season is
under way and there are eggs to be found. The second
is that you must not waste your time on the titmouse.
Even if you could make your way into the thorns, the
reward would not be worthwhile. Easier to find, and
much more substantial, are the eggs of the birds that
nest in the meadows.'

'Like the skylark?' suggested Blaze.

'Mmm ....' The old fox licked his lips. 'The eggs of
the lark are not to be passed by, but they too are small.
Much more satisfying are the eggs of the peewit or the
duck — or, better still, the eggs of the goose or the swan.
But then, the bigger the eggs, the more dangerous it is
to take them.'

'And Hop-along says they mustn't cross the river,'
said She-la, taking the opportunity to remind the old
fox of what she had told him.

'That's right,' the old fox confirmed. 'You mustn't
cross the river. I hear Hop-along has told you there are
some strange creatures over there — so be warned.'

Whether Old Sage Brush believed that there were
such dangers on the other side of the river, She-la
didn't know, but she was grateful for the warning he
had given to the cubs.

In the days that followed, the cubs spent much of
their time in the meadows, looking for the eggs that the
old fox had told them about. The nest of the lark, they
discovered, was a difficult one to find. Even though the
lark seemed to sing and hover above it, it was never
where they imagined it might be. Easier to find was the
nest of the peewit. The eggs had dark blotches that
made them difficult to see against the dark, peaty soil,
but they were, as the old fox had told them, quite big.

Soon the cubs had become quite adept at finding the

eggs of ground-nesting birds, and had learned not to be fooled when a bird pretended to be injured in an effort to draw them away from its nest. Old Sage Brush heard of these things with quiet satisfaction and was happy with their progress — until, one day, they returned in a state of great excitement to tell him they had found an egg as big as a turnip. It was then he realised that the cubs had ignored Hop-along's warnings not to cross the river, and that some of the things Hop-along had said he had seen might not have been figments of his imagination.

3

Picking Up the Pieces

Old Sage Brush made his way down through the fields. As he passed through a row of beech trees, he stopped and listened to the wind. A short distance beyond the trees, he stopped again. To a blind fox, the words of the great god Vulpes were all the more important. They were words which the old fox himself passed on to those who came to him enquiring about the secret of survival. 'Listen to the wind,' he always told them, 'for it shows you all you need to see.' To young and old, he would tell them, the wind was a friend — particularly to those who, like himself and Hop-along, had suffered at the hands of man.

Having satisfied himself that the wind held no hint

of danger, Old Sage Brush slipped beneath an arching briar and squeezed under a clump of gorse to emerge on the downward slope of a small quarry. It was a quarry for which man no longer had any use, and which was almost hidden from his view by a tangled growth of shrubbery. At the bottom of the quarry was a small cave which, the old fox knew, provided a dry den for two of his dearest friends. The vixen was at home and, as always, was delighted to see him.

The old fox had hardly settled himself when the other dog fox came in. He was unusual in that, alone among all the foxes in the valley, he had a black tip on his tail instead of a white one, a feature that had given him his name.

'Sage Brush!' he said. 'What brings you here?' The question was asked in a mixture of delight and surprise, because the old fox seldom strayed far from his home beneath the oak tree these days. Usually the other foxes went to see him.

'Black Tip,' said the old fox. 'I'm glad you're here.' Nosing around, he found a rabbit bone that still had some meat left on it. As he gnawed at it, the others waited, knowing that he would tell them what was on his mind in his own good time.

'It's Hop-along,' said Old Sage Brush finally. 'He's been telling some strange stories to the cubs.'

When he related what She-la had told him, the other two smiled and Black Tip said, 'He must have been dreaming.'

'Maybe it was something he ate,' suggested Vickey.

'I mean, birds with two necks, deer with two heads, pigs with two faces ... and a flower that eats rabbits!' Black Tip laughed. 'He must have been out of his mind.'

'Tall birds,' said the old fox. 'As tall as man, according to She-la.'

'And an animal that was neither fox nor cat, but a little bit of both?' Black Tip laughed again. 'There's no such thing.'

Old Sage Brush nodded. 'That's what I said.' He sighed. 'It's all very strange.'

'Have you spoken to Hop-along yourself?' asked Vickey.

'Not yet,' replied the old fox. 'Somehow I suspect he has told the cubs more than he would be prepared to tell any of us.'

'You think he's afraid we would laugh at him?' asked Vickey.

The old fox nodded. 'He wouldn't even discuss it with She-la.'

'So he had a dream,' said Black Tip. 'It wouldn't be the first time.'

'Perhaps,' suggested Vickey, 'it reflects his fears — you know, the fear that someday he may not be able to run fast enough to get out of danger.'

Old Sage Brush nodded. 'I said the very same thing to She-la. If you look with fearful eyes, you will see danger everywhere.'

'Or maybe it was something he just made up,' said Black Tip. 'You know, just to keep the cubs from straying too far.'

Black Tip and Vickey waited and wondered. Somehow, they felt the old fox wasn't telling them everything.

Old Sage Brush gnawed away at the bone. 'I found the story amusing too. But now the cubs tell me they've found a large egg, and I wonder.'

Black Tip stood up. 'Where?'

'I felt, when they told me, that they had disregarded Hop-along's instruction and crossed the river,' continued the old fox. 'And, sure enough, they admitted that they had. Somehow, Hop-along's story has aroused more curiosity in them than fear.'

Before Old Sage Brush could say anything more, two other foxes arrived. His daughter Sinnéad, and her mate, Skulking Dog, had picked up his scent and followed it to the quarry. As Sinnéad snuggled in beside Old Sage Brush, the others could see that the old fox was pleased that she had joined him. She was, after all, the only member of his family, apart from himself, to have escaped from man. Now she and her mate listened with fascination as Vickey and Black Tip related what the old fox had just told them.

When they had finished, Sinnéad looked up at her father and asked, 'What do you want us to do, then?'

The last time the old fox had actually seen his daughter, man had been probing their earth with long sticks to find out where they were. The sticks had blinded him, but he still remembered the little white patch on her forehead.

'Once before,' he told her, 'before we went to Man's Place, we considered the same question. It was agreed that Black Tip would be my eyes, Fang my strength, and Vickey my inspiration. Now you must all be my strength, my inspiration and, above all, my eyes. I want you to cross the river and find out what's going on. Look out for any strange tracks, and see if you can find that egg.'

'Maybe it's just a swan's egg,' suggested Skulking Dog.

The old fox nodded. 'If it is, so much the better. If it's not .... Well, then it would be a strange dream, wouldn't it?'

～

Rearing a family can be very wearing for a vixen, and Flame was in the process of recovering from the demands of her two cubs. As is the custom with foxes, Scat, her mate, had hunted for her during this period and would continue to do so until she was strong enough to hunt for herself. In the meantime, She-la was looking after the cubs, and Old Sage Brush had arranged with her that she would bring them to the meadows to meet the other four and show them where they had seen the large egg.

As the four made their way down to the meadows to meet the cubs, they were deep in thought. They heard the lark singing in the blue sky above them, and they heard the plaintive call of the peewit, but it was the egg of another bird that was uppermost in their minds. Perhaps the cubs were just exaggerating, they thought — maybe even playing a joke on adults who had told them stories about the weird and wonderful creatures they had come across in their travels. Well, they thought, they would soon find out.

Having handed the cubs over to the safe keeping of her friends, She-la made her way back towards the blackthorns. Black Tip told the cubs to lead the way, Vickey warned them not to go too far ahead, and they set off. It was, the adults felt, the oddest quest they had ever undertaken.

On crossing the river, they scanned the soft soil for any sign of the strange animal Hop-along claimed to have seen. They found the tracks of water-hens, coots and ducks, but nothing to indicate the presence of another fox, or a cat — and certainly no tracks that could have been left by an animal that was neither one nor the other.

Since Hop-along had been washed up on the bank, it followed that he had come down with the current, and it was no surprise to either Black Tip or his friends when the cubs made their way upriver. Here and there, various birds burst into flight at their approach, but the only long-legged bird they came across was the heron, and it stood its ground. It remained motionless in a shallow part of the river, its yellow-ringed eyes missing nothing that moved, either in the water rippling at its feet or on either bank.

After a while it became apparent that Blaze and Firefly were having difficulty finding their way, so Skulking Dog suggested that they should all fan out and scour the fields until they found the tracks the cubs had made on their earlier journey. This they did, and soon it was noticeable that the cubs were beginning to enjoy their outing. They romped around, looking for their tracks with great enthusiasm, and eventually their efforts were rewarded.

If the eyes of either man or beast had witnessed what followed, they would have wondered what the foxes were up to, for they began to wander all over the place. This was because they were following tracks which the cubs had made when they had been going nowhere in particular. The tracks went this way and that way, they doubled back and circled around, creating a tangle that reflected the frolics of cubs who had been exploring the world — its plants and flowers, its bees and birds, its scents and sights — for the very first time.

No wonder, then, that the foxes seemed to wander all over the place. However, they persevered, and eventually the tracks led them to a small copse of trees at a bend in the river. The ground was very marshy, and man had dumped some of his rubbish on it. The result was a smell which was so offensive to the foxes' sensitive noses, it dulled for a moment their ability to sense other smells.

The offensive odour, in fact, was not all attributable to the rubbish that man had dumped, but, as they were about to discover, was also due to other things that had been discarded within the copse. Leading the way, Blaze and Firefly turned and looked at their elders in triumph. For there, beneath the sweeping branches, was the broken shell of a large egg. It was larger than any egg the others had ever seen before. Indeed, one half of the shell — the biggest piece to remain intact — contained enough rainwater to slake the thirst of several foxes.

Skulking Dog — who, for many seasons, had specialised in raiding farmyards for hens and scouring the meadows for duck eggs — sniffed the soil beneath the shell to see if he could identify the bird that had laid it. Puzzled, he shook his head and stepped back so that some of the others could try. His mate, Sinnéad, was next, then Vickey and Black Tip. They too failed to identify it. The contents of the egg, they could see, had soaked into the soil and were contributing to the smell of the rubbish and the dank vegetation that was all around them.

'I don't suppose a swan could have been nesting in here?' said Vickey.

Black Tip shook his head. 'Swans always build their nests on the river-bank, or down in the lake.'

'It's too big to be a swan's egg,' said Sinnéad.

'And anyway,' observed Skulking Dog, 'there's no sign of a nest. It looks as if the egg has just been left here.'

'But who would have done that?' wondered Black Tip. 'Crows wouldn't have been able to bring it in here. Or magpies.'

'And it would have been much too big for a stoat to roll in,' said Skulking Dog.

'Or a hedgehog,' said Vickey.

Black Tip nodded. 'Sure, it's as big as a hedgehog. Bigger, even!'

'And even a hedgehog wouldn't have been able to break it open,' said Skulking Dog. 'Look how thick it is.'

Sinnéad bent down to sniff again. 'Anyway, the yolk hasn't been eaten. It's just soaked into the soil.'

'You're right,' said Black Tip. 'So what kind of egg is it, and how did it come to be here?'

All this time, the cubs had remained quiet. 'Perhaps,' said Blaze, 'it was laid by the big bird Hop-along saw.'

'The one he said was as tall as man,' added Firefly. 'The one with two long legs and two long necks.'

Vickey smiled patiently at them, saying, 'There's no such thing.'

'Then what did lay it?' asked Blaze.

Black Tip was about to say something when Firefly began to wriggle and scream.

'What's wrong?' asked Skulking Dog, bounding forward.

'It's my tail,' cried Firefly. 'It's stuck!'

The others saw that, while the two cubs had been standing listening, Firefly had draped her tail over a large, pink, hairy leaf. The hairs on the leaf were long and sticky, and her tail had stuck to them. Now, as she struggled to pull herself clear, the leaf folded over as if to grasp her tail more tightly.

Seeing her predicament, the other foxes rushed to her assistance. Skulking Dog, who was nearest to her, caught her by the scruff of the neck and began to pull. She didn't budge. Fearing that she was going to be swallowed up by the plant, the others also caught her and began to pull. Bit by bit, they dragged her clear, and, as the leaf opened up again, they saw that it contained a number of undigested bones.

'Rabbit bones!' gasped Vickey.

'So Hop-along wasn't making it up,' said Sinnéad.

Looking up, they saw that the leaves belonged to what seemed to be a giant daisy. And now, for the first time, they also saw that they weren't in a copse of trees, but in a clump of overgrown weeds.

'What do you think we should do?' asked Vickey.

Black Tip looked around for anything else that might be a danger to them and whispered, 'Before we go any further, I think we should report back to Old Sage Brush.'

The others looked around at their strange surroundings and nodded.

'Come on, Firefly,' said Vickey. 'You can wash your tail when we're crossing the river.'

As they made their way back through the meadows, the cubs raced ahead. Firefly was anxious to rid her tail of the sticky substance that made it look so thin, and to fluff it out into the modest brush that showed she was beginning to develop into a young fox. Both were also anxious to relate their experience to their parents, to Hop-along and She-la, and indeed to anyone else who would listen to them up in the blackthorns.

Old Sage Brush was a better listener than most, and he listened intently to what Vickey and her friends had to report. One by one, bit by bit, they told him exactly what they had seen and what had happened. Knowing them of old, he knew they had a keen sense of observation and wouldn't exaggerate. Turning his sightless eyes to the sky, he stroked his grey whiskers now and then, and nodded and grunted, but didn't speak until they had said all they had to say.

'So Hop-along wasn't dreaming after all,' he said. 'I thought as much.'

'Firefly was lucky she wasn't swallowed up by ....' Vickey stopped.

'By a giant daisy?' said the old fox. 'Don't worry, I'm not going to laugh at you.'

'I can understand now why Hop-along was afraid to talk about it,' Vickey went on.

'But it's there, all right,' said Sinnéad. 'We saw it. And it was all we could do to pull Firefly away from it.'

Old Sage Brush nodded. 'Any sign of the bird that laid the egg?'

'No,' Black Tip informed him. 'No tracks. Nothing.'

'And this creature Hop-along spoke of — this half-fox-half-cat? Any sign of it?'

'Maybe he imagined that part of it,' suggested Skulking Dog.

'But he seems to think he saw its tracks,' Sinnéad reminded them.

'Maybe so,' said Black Tip. 'But we didn't see them.'

'Perhaps,' said the old fox, 'it's time we had a talk with Hop-along.' Turning to his daughter, he added, 'Sinnéad, would you go down to the blackthorns and tell him to come up and see me? She-la, too.'

'What about Scat and Flame?' asked Sinnéad.

'Bring them, too.'

A short time later, Hop-along hobbled into the earth beneath the oak tree and lay down beside them. She-la followed, and as she settled herself, she heard Old Sage Brush asking her mate, 'Why didn't you tell us what you saw on the other side of the river?'

'Because I don't know what I saw and what I didn't see.' Hop-along shifted uncomfortably, and it was obvious that his discomfort was in talking about his experience rather than the way he was settling himself. He shrugged and added, 'I don't know. Maybe it was something I ate. You see, I couldn't catch any rabbits. I mean, there were none to be found. So I started chewing anything I could find — mushrooms, beetles, that kind of thing.'

'You don't find mushrooms at this time of year,' the old fox reminded him.

'Well, maybe they were toadstools, or the stuff that grows on dead trees. I don't know, I was so hungry.'

Just then, Scat and Flame arrived, and Vickey told them, 'Your cubs have really started something, haven't they!'

Flame eased her body down. 'They're full of energy, all right.' She smiled and added, 'Which is more than I can say for myself. They've me worn out.'

'You're lucky to have She-la and Hop-along to look after them,' said Sinnéad.

'So who's looking after them now?' asked Vickey.

Flame looked at She-la, saying, 'I thought you were!'

At the same time She-la looked at Flame, saying, 'I thought you were!'

Realising that the cubs had now been on their own for some time, Flame got up and, despite the frailty of her condition, hurried back to the blackthorns, closely followed by She-la.

To their dismay, they found that the cubs had gone. Furthermore, their tracks showed that they had gone back to the river.

4

Across the River

Hearing a buzzing sound, Vickey shuffled over to a clump of wild arum that had pushed its way up through the withered grass beneath a hedge. Her long ears twitched and turned and told her the sound was coming from one of the central leaves, which had curled to form a deep, narrow cup. She peeped in and snorted when the leaf touched her nose, but she couldn't see the small flies she knew were trapped inside, so she crept back to where Old Sage Brush and Sinnéad were talking. Seeing a fly landing on a daisy, she nudged it with her nose, and as it flew off, she said, 'But I never saw a daisy catch anything, not even a small fly.'

Puzzled, Sinnéad looked at her and asked, 'What are you talking about?'

'Nothing,' said Vickey. 'It was just something Old Sage Brush told us when we were on our journey to Man's Place.'

'What was that?' asked the old fox.

'We were resting in the grounds of a big house, remember?' Old Sage Brush nodded, and Vickey went on, 'The undergrowth was thick, and there was a strong scent of pheasant in the wind. Somehow we felt so safe. Then you told us we couldn't stay.'

'Why not?' asked Sinnéad.

'Because we were in the Land of the Howling Dogs,' the old fox recalled.

Sinnéad shivered, and, sensing her unease, the old fox continued, 'That's right, you were lucky to get away from them.'

'And from man!' Sinnéad shivered again, saying, 'I really don't want to talk about it.'

'Anyway,' said Vickey, 'it was before you were rescued.' She paused before recalling, 'It was what Old Sage Brush said about one of the flowers.'

'What was that?' asked the old fox.

'You told us that, before man robbed you of your sight, you had watched small flies creeping into it, and that it had held them fast until they could carry away its pollen.'

Seeing Vickey still gazing at the daisy, Sinnéad asked, 'What sort of flower? You mean a daisy?'

Vickey shook her head. 'No, it was like that one over there, under the hedge.' Then she added, 'That's the point. I never saw a daisy catch a fly, even a small one.' She paused. 'I mean, an ordinary daisy. And yet, we saw one on the other side of the river that can catch a rabbit.'

'And very nearly a fox cub,' added Sinnéad. She sniffed the wind and, finding nothing to indicate that the searchers were returning, lowered her head onto her forepaws and wondered what was keeping them.

A short time later, Hop-along arrived and enquired if there was any news. Vickey shook her head and asked, 'Where's She-la?'

Hop-along settled himself somewhat awkwardly and told her, 'She's looking after Flame. Scat insisted on going with Black Tip and Skulking Dog to look for the cubs.'

'I told them not to come back until they found them,' said Old Sage Brush. 'Now, Hop-along, tell us more about what you saw.'

'Well,' said Hop-along, 'for a start, everything was a funny colour. Even the frogs. They were red.'

'Unless my memory deceives me,' the old fox told him, 'you sometimes see frogs with red blotches on their skin.'

'But these were completely red,' protested Hop-along. 'And they were everywhere. Really, I know it's hard to believe, but it was raining frogs.'

'Maybe they were just young frogs coming from the streams,' suggested Sinnéad.

'That's probably it,' said Vickey. 'When the time is right and it starts to rain, they can move out into the meadows in great numbers. Mind you, I've only seen it once myself. But if you're lucky enough to be in the right place at the right time, you can have a feast. One seems to hop out of the grass with every drop of rain.'

'There you are, then,' said the old fox. 'So it was raining frogs. What else?'

Before Hop-along could answer, Black Tip and Skulking Dog returned. Acting on Old Sage Brush's instructions, they had brought back the largest part of the eggshell, the half that had been filled with rain-water. As Skulking Dog placed it in front of the old fox, he explained that he had hardly been able to see where he was going when he was holding it in his mouth.

Hop-along hobbled over and sniffed the eggshell. 'Did you see any sign of the cubs?' he asked.

Black Tip shook his head. 'We followed their tracks a long way.'

'It appeared to me,' said Skulking Dog, 'that they were heading towards the Land of the Howling Dogs.'

'Poor Flame,' sighed Vickey. 'Have you told her?'

'Scat's gone to tell her,' said Black Tip.

'Did you see any of them?' asked Sinnéad. 'I mean, howling dogs?'

Skulking Dog shook his head. 'No — but then, you wouldn't expect to see them at this time of year.'

'At least that's some consolation,' said Sinnéad.

Old Sage Brush, who had listened without comment, was now moving his nose around the broken eggshell to find out how big it was. 'Still,' he said, 'if the size of this egg is anything to go by, there may be other dangers.'

'The bird with the long legs and the long neck,' said Black Tip.

'It had two long necks,' insisted Hop-along.

'One neck or two,' said Old Sage Brush, 'it's the legs that count. If they're as long as you say they are, they could outrun a fox, and I imagine they could be just as dangerous as a howling dog.'

'Sage Brush,' said Black Tip, 'when our cubs were growing up, you took them down to the river and showed them many things.'

'Mmm ....' said the old fox. 'You mean, things like eggshells?'

'That's right,' said Vickey. 'You showed them many

kinds of eggshells, and you told them how to read the signs so that they would know what had been feeding on them.'

Old Sage Brush smiled. 'So I did. So I did. I told them what to look for, so that they would know if the eggs had been broken by a stoat or a hedgehog, a crow or a magpie. But, sure, you know all that yourselves.'

'Of course we do,' said Black Tip. 'But you know more than we'll ever know. So maybe you can tell us what broke open this shell.'

'You told me yourselves, the first time you found it,' said the old fox, 'that the yolk had seeped into the soil. That being so, it's unlikely that it was broken open for what was inside it.'

'Why, then?' asked Skulking Dog.

Old Sage Brush brushed his whiskers with a fore-paw, as if to wipe away anything that had come from the eggshell. 'Well,' he told them, 'you said the shell wasn't in a nest. So it wasn't laid there. And it's too big to have been hidden there by any of our fellow creatures.' He took a deep breath and, breathing out through his nose, concluded, 'That means it must have been left there by man.'

'You mean it broke when he just threw it there?' asked Hop-along.

The old fox nodded. 'That seems the most likely explanation. As you know, man is wasteful. The creatures of the wild are not. We will not discard food so readily. Yet man seems to think we are lesser beings than he is. But are we?' He paused before adding, 'Man, for example, can break an egg, but can he put it back together again?'

Sinnéad smiled. 'No one can do that.'

The old fox looked at his daughter, and even though he could not see her, it was a look of great affection.

'Man cannot put an egg back together,' he told her. 'But there is one creature that can. A creature he has very little regard for.'

'You mean just the shells,' asked Black Tip, 'or the whole egg, yolk and all?'

'The whole egg,' replied the old fox. 'Yolk and all.'

Skulking Dog laughed. 'We can't do it, and we're smarter than most. In fact, it takes us all our time to get the yolk *out*.'

'True,' said Old Sage Brush. 'There are many things we can do that man cannot do, but putting an egg back together again is not one of them.'

'Which creature, then?' asked Sinnéad. Her father shook his head, and she nudged him, saying, 'Which creature can put an egg back together again? Go on, tell us.'

'No,' the old fox replied. 'I won't tell you. All I will say is, it can be done. Try and work it out for yourselves.'

Before they could discuss the matter further, a voice from the long grass nearby said, 'The birds can't fly and the rats can't run.'

Startled, they turned their heads to find out who was speaking, but it was Old Sage Brush who recognised the voice first.

'Ratwiddle!' he exclaimed, in a mixture of surprise and amusement. 'We didn't know you were there.'

Ratwiddle got up and, with his head cocked to one side as if he had a crick in his neck that made him gaze up at the sky, moved to another patch of long grass. Lying down, but still looking up at the sky, he said, 'The birds can't fly and the rats can't run. Cock-a-doodle-do.' He paused, then added, 'Two heads are worse than one.'

Vickey got up and went over to him. 'Ratwiddle,'

she said, 'have you seen these strange creatures, the ones Hop-along has been telling us about?'

Ignoring her, Ratwiddle continued to look up at the sky, in such a way that it seemed his mind was away up there somewhere too.

'It's no use,' said Vickey, as she returned to the others. 'You might as well be talking to the trees.'

At the same time, Ratwiddle got up. As he veered away at an uncanny angle, he said, 'Catch the rabbits if you can, but don't eat the rats.'

'Don't mind him,' said Black Tip. 'His mind has been addled by all the rats he catches down in the meadows.'

'Still,' said Hop-along, 'he must have been on the far side of the river. He knows the rabbits are gone. And he must have seen that strange bird — the one with the long legs. I doubt very much if it can fly.'

Sinnéad sniggered. 'It's just as well, or it would be picking a few of us up for its supper.'

'And he said two heads are worse than one,' recalled Hop-along. 'It sounds to me as if he has seen some of the things that I saw.'

'Ratwiddle often speaks of things he sees only in the depths of his own tormented mind,' said Old Sage Brush. 'You know that as well as I do. Unfortunately, some of the things he says turn out to be true.'

'What do you think we should do?' asked Vickey.

The old fox raised his grey-whiskered nose in the air and breathed deeply. 'I think,' he said, 'it's time we went across the river to see for ourselves.'

'What do you mean, *we*?' asked Vickey.

'*We*,' replied Old Sage Brush. 'Me and you and the rest of us. Why, do you think I'm too old to go with you?'

'No, I ....' Vickey shifted uncomfortably as she searched for words that wouldn't offend the old fox.

'It's just that you're not as strong as you used to be, and it could be dangerous.'

'Vickey's right,' said Black Tip, 'it could be very dangerous. I mean, if the bird that laid that egg is half as big as Hop-along seems to think it is, we could all be in trouble.'

'All right, all right,' said the old fox. 'I know I'm not as young as I used to be. But as my body has grown weak, my mind has grown strong. And in times of trouble, my mind is more important to me than my legs.'

'Not if you have to run for your life,' argued Skulking Dog.

Old Sage Brush smiled. 'You do the running. You, and Sinnéad, Black Tip and Vickey.' Skulking Dog was about to say something, but the old fox cut him short. 'I know, I know — it's not in our nature to run in packs. But sometimes it's safer. We've done it before and we can do it again. Hop-along and She-la will stay with me. We'll follow at a safe distance.'

'But why?' asked Sinnéad. 'Why put yourself and Hop-along in danger?'

Old Sage Brush was pleased that his daughter should be so concerned, but he assured her, 'If you go ahead, what danger can there be for us? Anyway, I'm curious to see the place where you found this egg — and to find out more about the bird that laid it. And the only way I can do that is through the eyes of the fox that has seen it. Now, off you go. Hop-along and I will make haste, but with a little more caution.'

Vickey and Sinnéad exchanged smiles. They knew there was no point in arguing further with the old fox, so they joined their mates and set off, Vickey trotting along beside Black Tip, Sinnéad beside Skulking Dog.

Beyond the row of beech trees, they came across

Flame. She was standing outside the blackthorns, looking anxiously down at the river for any sign of her cubs.

'No sign of them?' asked Vickey.

Flame shook her head. 'No.'

'Well, we're going to have another look for them,' Black Tip told her, 'and we won't come back until we find them.'

'And that's a promise,' added Skulking Dog.

'Anyway,' said Sinnéad, 'from what I know of Blaze and Firefly, they're well able to look after themselves.'

'That's what I've been telling her,' said Scat, emerging from the blackthorns. 'They're weaned now, and they can run as fast as the rest of us.'

Black Tip smiled. 'Maybe even faster.'

Black Tip's words, like those of his friends, were meant to reassure, but Flame, they could see, was not to be reassured. She stood tense and unsmiling, her weak legs trembling as she gazed down at the river and beyond.

'Hop-along and She-la are coming too,' said Vickey. 'Well, at a safe distance.'

'Old Sage Brush insisted on coming,' explained Sinnéad. 'So they'll follow on with him.'

For the first time, Flame smiled and nodded. The old fox's decision to tag along, they could see, meant a lot to her. But still she continued to gaze at the river and beyond. If that was where her cubs were, then that was where her mind was, and it would stay there until they were found.

'Come on,' said Black Tip. 'The sooner we go, the sooner we'll find them.'

'Thanks,' said Scat, but the others had gone. Racing down the fields, they wended their way through the rushy meadows. As they passed, birds of all shapes and sizes rose from their nesting-places and flew down towards the lake. Instinctively, Skulking Dog paused and looked up, knowing that where there were birds' nests there was food. However, he quickly caught up with the others, and they didn't stop until they reached the river.

When the time had come for foxes to have their cubs, their fur had lost its sheen and the trappers who hunted them for their fur had put away their snares. However, sheep were also having their young, and farmers, anxious not to lose any lambs to the fox, had put out their snares. For this reason, the foxes heading north along the river kept to the meadows as long as they could. At the bend in the river, they glanced over at the cluster of giant weeds where they had found the egg, left a mark for Old Sage Brush to indicate which way they were going, and took cover on a small hill covered with hazel bushes.

'We must be careful,' warned Black Tip. 'Just because we didn't come across any choking hedge-traps the last time, it doesn't mean we won't run into them now. So we'll try and keep to places like this. Places man has no use for.'

'Or Cow Pasture,' said Skulking Dog. 'Or the Land of the Horse. But not Sheep Land.'

The vixens nodded in agreement, but Sinnéad was worried. 'And what about the Land of the Howling Dogs?' she asked. 'How can we avoid that?'

'I told you before,' said Skulking Dog. 'The howling dogs are locked up. They don't come out until the frost comes on the ground. You know that as well as I do.'

'Maybe so,' said Sinnéad, 'but sometimes man brings the young dogs out and gives them a taste of blood — the blood of our cubs.'

'Sometimes,' Vickey agreed. 'But he isn't going to let the howling dogs run through his crops.'

'And he can't stop us from doing so,' said Black Tip. 'All we have to do is follow the tracks his machines have left.'

'The crops are high enough to hide us,' said Skulking Dog, 'and man never leaves any choking hedge-traps in them. He's only interested in chasing off the crows.'

Off they went again, and, by using various paths and places where they wouldn't be seen, the two dog foxes led their mates to the land where Blaze and Firefly had gone.

It was a land in which there was an occasional big house, surrounded by tall trees and open fields, where horses galloped in the sun or grazed contentedly behind white wooden railings.

Settling down in the rich profusion of undergrowth near one of the houses, Vickey looked up at the giant hogweed and at the trees above, where rooks were swirling around in great numbers. Somehow she had a feeling she had been there before, but she couldn't remember when.

Having rested, they circled around behind the house, using the undergrowth as cover, and kept going across the fields until they came to another big house. Unlike the previous one, this one looked as if man might have deserted it. Then, as they got the scent of the weeds on the front lawn, Sinnéad began to shiver.

'I've been here before,' she said. 'This is the Land of the Howling Dogs.'

'So it is,' said Vickey, remembering now why the area had seemed familiar to her.

Skulking Dog nodded. This, he realised, was where he and another fox had helped Sinnéad escape from the howling dogs.

Sinnéad lay down. She was still shivering, and she said, 'I don't want to go any further. I want to go back.'

'We can't go back now,' protested Black Tip. 'At least, not until we find Blaze and Firefly.'

As they wondered what to do, a strange sound came to their ears. Was it the cry of the howling dogs? they wondered. Or was it simply the crow of a cock? Or was it something else? They were about to turn tail and run when Skulking Dog said, 'We can't go back without the cubs. We promised.'

'Vickey,' said Black Tip, 'you take Sinnéad back to the trees where we stopped for a rest. You should be safe there. We'll go ahead and see if we can find the cubs.'

Vickey nodded. 'All right, but be careful.'

Black Tip assured her they would, and as soon as the two vixens had gone, he and Skulking Dog made their way cautiously around the side of the big house. There was no sign of man, but they could still hear strange sounds coming from somewhere beyond the trees at the back. The yard, they could see, was over-grown with nettles, and as they made their way down a path beneath the trees, they found that colonies of ants had made their homes beneath many of the flag-stones. From countless holes and crevices, hordes of the little creatures were coming and going, in a frenzy of activity that indicated it wouldn't be long before they sprouted wings and took to the air.

Beyond the trees, the path opened out into a cart-track. At the end of that, a man in a white coat had put down two buckets and was opening the gate of a field enclosed by a high wire fence.

'Look!' exclaimed Black Tip.

'I see him,' whispered Skulking Dog.

'Not him,' said Black Tip. 'Look what's in the field!'

Hardly able to believe their eyes, the two foxes stood looking at the strangest collection of creatures they had ever seen. Beyond the gate was a tall, greyish-brown bird. It had two long necks and two heads, which, when raised, were higher than the man, and both heads were waiting to be fed. Also waiting to be fed were a deer with a head at each end, a pig with two faces, and a sheep with a horn where it should have had a tail. They made all sorts of hungry noises as they waited for the man with the buckets to come through.

Then, from a bare tree in the middle of the enclosure, came a piercing screech and a loud 'cock-a-doodle-do'. Looking up, the foxes saw a large bird leaving the tree and gliding down to the gate. As it landed, they thought it looked like a rainbow bird, but when it fanned out its tail, they could see that the feathers didn't have the colours of the rainbow. Furthermore, the bird wiggled its large tail and, to their amazement, seemed to disappear.

But there, plain to be seen, were Blaze and Firefly. The cubs were higher up the tree that the bird had just left, and they were clinging on for dear life.

5

The Cycle of Life

Stunned by what they had seen, Black Tip and Skulking Dog beat a hasty retreat to the safety of the farm buildings. As they skirted around these, the smell of rat came to their nostrils, and, following it up, they discovered several dead rats lying on the floor of an open shed.

Skulking Dog rushed over and was about to pick up one of the rats when Black Tip stopped him. 'Remember what Ratwiddle said? "Catch the rabbits if you can, but don't eat the rats."'

Skulking Dog pulled his head back as sharply as if he had been stung by a wasp. 'You're right. He also said, "the birds can't fly and the rats can't run."'

'"Cock-a-doodle-do,"' added Black Tip. '"Two heads are worse than one."'

'So he must have been here,' said Skulking Dog. 'But I wonder what he meant when he said, "Don't eat the rats."'

One or two of the rats, they could see, had been dead for a long time and were only skin and bone. However, the one Skulking Dog had been about to pick up had not been dead for very long. Wondering what had killed them, both foxes looked around. There was a pile of potatoes in the shed, and the rats had been gnawing at some of them, but there was nothing unusual in that.

'Maybe they've been poisoned,' suggested Black Tip.

'That's it,' exclaimed Skulking Dog. 'They must have been poisoned. The last time I was here — the time we rescued Sinnéad — this place was overrun with rats and mice. Man must have laid out poison for them. But how did Ratwiddle know?'

Black Tip shrugged. 'How does he know any of the things he says? But then, he's always hunting rats down in the meadows. That's what has him the way he is.'

'Sometimes he seems to know an awful lot more than we do, all right,' Skulking Dog agreed. 'And it's just as well he warned us about the rats, or I'd be poisoned too.'

'It's a wonder the cubs didn't pick one up,' said Black Tip. 'And how are we going to get them out of there?'

'Did you ever see such creatures?' asked Skulking Dog. 'I'm not surprised Hop-along thought he was seeing things.'

A long line of ants came marching up out of a crevice in the floor, and Skulking Dog was about to devour them when it occurred to him that maybe they had eaten some of the poison too. Maybe, he thought, it hadn't affected them the way it had affected the rats, but was still in their bodies, for ants were peculiar little insects. Nothing seemed to stop them.

'Listen,' warned Black Tip. 'It's man. He's coming back to the house.'

Skulking Dog lifted his head. He too had heard the banging of the gate and the rattle of the bar as the man closed it. 'What do you think we should do?' he asked.

'There's nothing we can do,' Black Tip replied. 'The cubs are in there and we're out here. I think we should collect the vixens and return to Old Sage Brush.'

Skulking Dog nodded. 'Maybe he'll know what to do.'

Leading the way, She-la had followed the others as far as the river, but then they had had to go back up along it for a considerable distance before she could find a place that was shallow enough for Hop-along and Old Sage Brush to cross. On the far side, she picked up the others' scent again and followed it until they came to the bend in the river. Hop-along immediately recognised the clump of giant weeds that he had mistaken for a small copse of trees. Even now, in the clear light of day, he could not accept that he had seen a daisy so large it had eaten a rabbit.

'What's the matter?' asked She-la.

Before Hop-along could answer, Old Sage Brush said to him, 'This is it, isn't it? Where you followed the rabbit?' He had felt the tremble run through Hop-along's body.

'I thought at first I must have imagined it,' said Hop-along.

'What's that awful smell?' asked She-la.

Old Sage Brush put his nose up into the wind and sniffed. 'Rotting eggs, rotting bones, rotting vegetation, I imagine.'

'Man has dumped a lot of rubbish in here, all right,' She-la told him. Then, seeing a pile of rotting potatoes, she added, 'Do you remember the flowers of the fields — the ones he withers with spray and then collects the roots?' When the old fox nodded, she went on, 'He has dumped a lot of those as well. Some of them have rotted and some have begun to grow.' She looked up and wondered, 'But why is everything growing so tall? The thistles, the ragwort — they're nearly as tall as trees.'

'I thought they *were* trees,' said Hop-along. 'It was only when I took a closer look that I saw what they were.'

'And what about the flowers that are on them?' Old Sage Brush asked him. 'You said they were different.'

'They *were* different,' Hop-along asserted. Tilting his head back as far as it would go, he looked up at the tops of the giant weeds. The seed-heads of the thistles, he could see, were purple, the trumpets of the bindweed were white. 'But it must have been my imagination,' he added. 'They're the same colours they always are.'

She-la, who was also straining her neck to see the tops of the weeds, remarked, 'But they're huge. And they've flowered before their time.'

'What's that buzzing noise?' asked Old Sage Brush. 'Is it bees?'

'No,' She-la told him. 'It's flies. They're all over the place.'

The old fox nodded. He was trying to see it all in his

mind's eye, but, never having seen anything like it before he lost his sight, he found it difficult to imagine. 'Thistles as tall as trees? Daisies that eat rabbits? It's not natural,' he said at last. 'It must be man's work.' He sniffed again and added, 'As I said before, man can break an egg, but he can't put it together again. Now, I suspect, he has done something else he may not be able to undo.'

'What do you mean?' asked Hop-along.

Old Sage Brush shook his head. 'I don't really know. All I know is that man is always breaking the laws of nature. More often than not, nature will repair the damage. But this time, I fear, man may have gone too far.'

Like all foxes, both Hop-along and his mate had witnessed the damage man continued to inflict on the countryside. They had seen him cut down the hedges and burn them. They had seen him dredge the rivers, leaving them so bare that nothing could live in them. They had even seen him kill the flowers of the fields so that the bees had to go elsewhere to find their pollen. But what the old fox meant by suggesting that now, perhaps, man had gone too far, they did not know. All they knew was that they were looking at something they did not understand, and it frightened them.

Hop-along hobbled up beside She-la. 'The daisy, or whatever it is,' he said. 'The one I saw eating the rabbit. It's in the middle of all this. Do you want to see it?'

She-la shivered. 'No, thanks. I think we should be moving on.'

'So do I,' said Old Sage Brush. 'The smell of this place is so strong I can't pick up anything else — even the scent of our friends, or the scent of danger.'

Soon the odour that had offended their senses of smell was left behind, and they came across the mark that told them which way the other foxes had gone. A short distance further on, they stopped on a small hill covered with hazel trees. From the scents and the way the long grass was flattened, they knew the others had also stopped there.

Old Sage Brush was tired, and he decided they would wait on the Hill of Hazels until the others returned. Perhaps it was because their senses of smell had been dulled somewhat, but none of them — not even the old fox — realised that, while they had been following the scent of the other foxes, another creature had been following them. As a result, it wasn't until some time later that they got the first hint of danger.

A gentle breeze was blowing across the hill, waving the long grass this way and that, as the three foxes rested. Hop-along was dozing, wondering vaguely how an egg could be broken and then put together again. Somehow, it didn't seem possible. Then he found himself thinking once more about the tall two-headed bird, and all the other strange things he had seen on his travels.

Seeing Hop-along's body twitch and shiver, She-la got up and lay down beside him. She knew he was still tormented by whatever he had seen, and suddenly she felt a great loneliness come upon her. It was, she realised, a loneliness caused by the fact that she was responsible for the safety of her two companions. One was lame, the other blind. If the worst came to the worst, what could she do?

Old Sage Brush was lying with his nose raised, his ears cocked, listening to the wind and what it had to say. At first it told him nothing; but then, as it blew away the smells of man's work in the meadow, it brought him something else besides the scent of fox. Yet it was fox of a kind — or was it cat? Not being able to identify it to his satisfaction, he roused Hop-along and asked him if he recognised it.

She-la was on her feet now too, but it was her mate who spoke first.

'That's it,' said Hop-along, and he began to shake again. 'The creature I was telling you about. I've smelt it before. And I've seen it. It's got the nose of a fox, but it has the eyes of a cat!'

'Do you think we should make a run for it?' asked She-la.

Old Sage Brush shook his head. 'She-la,' he said, 'I have never doubted your courage. Nor has Hop-along. We both know you would do your best to lead us to safety. But, whatever it is out there, it would soon realise that we were not in a position to outrun it. And what would happen if one of us got separated or fell behind?'

Hop-along was standing beside his mate. His body was quivering and he was obviously very agitated. 'What will we do, then?' he asked.

'We won't do anything,' said the old fox.

'But we can't just stay here and do nothing,' Hop-along protested.

'Why not?' said Old Sage Brush. 'The creature — whatever it is — will know from our scent that there are several of us. However, it will not know how many, nor will it know that one of us has only three paws and that another is blind. No, there is safety in numbers, and I think it will be safer to stay where we are.'

Fearful of what might happen to them, Hop-along lowered himself down into the long grass. Unlike Old Sage Brush, he had looked into the eyes of the creature that was stalking them, and it was with great apprehension that he accepted the logic of what the old fox had said.

Old Sage Brush closed his sightless eyes and, from the inner darkness of his mind, listened intently. From what Hop-along had told him, he could imagine what the creature that was stalking them might look like. He also knew, from the faint suggestion of scent that came and went with the wind, that it was circling the hill as it tried to assess how many of them there were. But it made no sound, not even the crack of a twig as it picked its way among the bushes, and he knew it was a stealthy hunter.

Hardly daring to breathe, the three foxes lay still and listened. Rotating their long black ears, and occasionally turning their heads, they endeavoured to follow the movements of the creature that circled the hill below them. Bit by bit, they knew, it was coming closer and closer.

Then, as he scanned the darkness beneath the bushes, Hop-along found himself looking into its eyes once more.

'It's watching us,' he whispered. 'Over there, under the bushes.'

When She-la looked, however, the eyes that had peered at them from beneath the bushes had gone. Hop-along, she saw, was trembling more than ever, and she was about to say they should make a run for it when something came crashing through the bushes towards them. All three were on their feet, about to run for their lives, when She-la cried, 'It's all right! It's all right — it's Black Tip.'

Greatly relieved, Old Sage Brush and Hop-along followed She-la back to where they had been lying. 'We thought it was that creature Hop-along told us about,' explained Old Sage Brush. 'The one that's ....'

'Half-fox, half-cat,' Black Tip finished. 'I know. We got the scent of it when we arrived at the bottom of the hill. The others have gone after it.'

'I saw it,' said Hop-along. 'It was circling the hill. It was stalking us. And then I saw it looking at us from under the bushes.'

Seeing that Hop-along was still trembling, Black Tip assured him, 'Well, it's gone now, and if the others catch up with it, it won't be stalking any more.'

A short time later, the others returned. They had, they said, followed the creature as far as the meadows, but then they had lost its scent.

'Did you see it?' asked Old Sage Brush.

'Not really,' Skulking Dog told him. 'It must have taken off before we arrived.'

'It probably heard us coming,' added Sinnéad.

She-la smiled. 'I'm not surprised. You made enough noise.'

'Once we picked up its scent,' said Vickey, 'we decided to make as much noise as we could.'

'Just in case you might be in trouble,' explained Black Tip. 'We thought it would be better to try and scare it off.'

'It's just as well you did.' Hop-along, who was only now beginning to regain his composure, gave a hollow laugh. 'But you nearly scared the wits out of us.'

Between them, Black Tip and Skulking Dog described all that they had seen — the bird with two necks, the deer with two heads, the pig with two faces, the sheep with a horn where it should have had a tail.

'So I did see them!' exclaimed Hop-along. 'I did see them!'

'It's all very strange,' said Vickey. 'And ants getting ready to swarm at this time of year .... It's not natural.'

'Never mind the ants,' said She-la. 'What about the cubs?'

'They're in the middle of the strange creatures we

saw in the pen,' Black Tip told her. As she jumped to her feet, he added, 'But they're all right. They're up a tree. The creatures can't get at them.'

She-la settled down again, and Hop-along asked, 'How did they end up in there?'

'The question is,' said Old Sage Brush, 'not how they got there, but how we are going to get them out.'

'Do you think that other creature came from there?' asked Hop-along. 'The one that was stalking us?'

'Seems likely,' said Black Tip. 'Maybe it was in there too, but managed to escape.'

'But how?' asked the old fox. 'How did it escape? And how can we help the cubs to escape?'

It was only now, as Skulking Dog and Black Tip related their encounter with the rats, that they realised none of them had eaten for some time. The absence of rabbits in the area was, they had discovered, not Hop-along's imagination either. The rabbits were in their burrows, all right, but they were not coming out. Whether this was because of the activities of the fox-cat, or because of the presence of so many foxes on the hill, they didn't know, and they didn't feel like waiting too long to find out.

'There are other things besides rabbits,' said Old Sage Brush. 'If it was raining frogs, they must still be around. And if Hop-along saw one long-tailed field mouse, then there must be more. But a water hen — or, better still, a pheasant — would be a lot better.'

'But we'd better stay away from the rats,' warned Skulking Dog. 'At least until we find out what's going on.'

The vixens volunteered to do the hunting, and as the others waited for them to return, Hop-along's thoughts returned to the large eggshell he had found in the meadow.

'Sage Brush,' he said, 'you told us that man can break an egg but cannot put it together again.' When the old fox grunted, he went on, 'You also said that man is always breaking the laws of nature.' Old Sage Brush nodded, and Hop-along asked, 'Do you think that maybe the hatching of a bird with two heads is man's work?'

'In nature,' replied the old fox, 'everything takes its course. Just as the seasons take their course, so do birth, life and death. The birth of our young, the buds on the branches, the growth of a fox, the spread of a tree, the moult of our fur, the fall of the leaves, the frailty of age, the ebbing of sap. Everything is in its place, and that is as it should be. But when man interferes with nature, then the cycle of life is broken and things go wrong.'

Old Sage Brush stroked his grey whiskers and thought for a moment. 'Perhaps,' he continued, 'man thinks that a bird with two heads might be better than a bird with one. But then, it takes twice as much to feed two heads as it takes to feed one. And what would happen if a bird with two heads got a mate with two heads? You might end up with a bird that has four heads. How would you feed a bird with four heads? And who could say it would end there? Fortunately, these are things that do not trouble the creatures of the wild. We are content with things as they are. But, from what you have seen, it would appear that man is not.'

The other foxes found it difficult to understand the wisdom of what Old Sage Brush was saying, but they knew that when litters were too big, food could become scarce, so they nodded and grunted as if they understood. Nor could they imagine how they were going to rescue the cubs from their predicament.

After a while, the vixens returned with bits and

pieces of food, and they were all enjoying these when another creature came crashing through the bushes. Thinking it was the fox-cat, they instinctively dropped their food and scattered in all directions — only to find that it was Ratwiddle. Sheepishly, they returned and picked up their food while their unexpected visitor, in his customary fashion, lay down nearby and, in a way that seemed to ignore them, looked up at the sky.

Knowing it was pointless trying to talk to Ratwiddle, Skulking Dog turned to the others. 'We're going to have to put our own heads together, if we're to figure out how to get Blaze and Firefly out of there,' he told them.

'It's going to rain flies,' said Ratwiddle, to no one in particular. He was still looking up at the sky, which, the others could see, was cloudless and held no sign of rain.

Black Tip shook his head. 'It's a pity Ratwiddle can't talk sense to us. I think he knows a lot more about that place than we do.'

Old Sage Brush nodded. 'Well, maybe, in his own strange way, he is talking sense.'

'How do you mean?' asked Vickey.

Old Sage Brush swallowed his food and replied, 'Well, what he has just said has given me an idea. If a plague of frogs can give food to Hop-along, then maybe, just maybe, another plague can come to the aid of the cubs.'

6

A Plague of Flies

When Sinnéad felt she had been to the big house before, she was right, and when Old Sage Brush thought that what Black Tip and Skulking Dog had seen there was the work of man, he wasn't far wrong.

It had been several seasons since Sinnéad, in her flight from the howling dogs, had taken refuge at the big house. At that time, scientists had been using it to explore alternative sources of energy, as oil-producing countries in the Middle East had pushed up their prices. In the lawns of the house, they had tried to find ways of harnessing the rays of the sun, but, in a country that had less sunshine than it would have liked, their experiments had yielded little. And so the big house had fallen into disuse — until the man in the white coat had come there to carry out experiments of a different nature.

The man had worked for a reputable firm that was exploring what it believed would be the benefits of genetically modified food. However, he had been sloppy in his work. This had led to costly mistakes, and he had been let go. He had then set up his own laboratory in the big house. There, in the secrecy of the countryside, he had begun work on his own ideas — ideas which reputable firms might well have regarded with great suspicion, as they centred around an invention he called a gene machine.

Like many other scientists, the man who had come to the big house had spent a lot of time manipulating the genetic codes of certain food plants, including potatoes and cereals. The aim was to endow them with superior qualities that would make them more resistant to the weed-killers and pesticides used to kill thistles, beetles and other unwanted visitors. However, tests with rats and mice had shown that, even with his gene machine, he had failed to make the breakthrough he had hoped for. Some of the animals had wasted and died after being fed with the modified plants. So he had approached the problem of insects from a different angle.

For some time the man had studied the insect-eating plants that grow in the bogs of the west of Ireland, including the sundew and butterwort, and he had selected the sundew for his experiments. He had spent many hours observing this plant, which has a white flower like a daisy and gets its name from the fact that, even in the sunniest of weather, its leaves seem to be covered with dew. On closer examination, he could see that the leaves got their dewy appearance from tiny hairs, each of which carried a glistening bead that looked like a droplet of water. These attracted thirsty insects, which didn't discover until it was too late that they were not water, but a glue-like secretion that held them fast. When a large insect, such as the damsel fly, was captured, the man sometimes saw the whole leaf fold over, smothering the victim and trapping it until the plant's digestive juices got to work. If these plants could be grown on the fringes of fields of corn and other cereals, he reasoned, they would devour many of the insects that damaged such crops, lessening the need for pesticides.

With this in mind, the errant scientist had not only collected samples of sundew plants from the bogs of Connemara, but also obtained larger specimens of the same family from some of the more exotic parts of the world. By mixing them in his machine, he had manipulated their genes in an effort to produce a sturdier plant. However, he had overlooked the fact that sundews had become insect-eaters because the bogs in which they grew were so impoverished that they had difficulty extracting enough nutrients to survive. They were not at all suited to the rich farmlands in which he had tried to grow them, and when they had failed, so had his experiment.

So it was that the man in the white coat had heaped failure upon failure. With the same sloppiness that had cost him his job, he had thrown aside the by-products of his flawed research — including the potatoes and the sundews, the thistles and the other weeds — and turned to yet another project.

Perhaps it was because his head was always bent over a microscope, or because he wasn't as observant as a scientist should be, but he had failed to notice that something odd had occurred. Like the superbug that had evolved in hospitals in response to all the antibiotics that were being used, some of the plants — including the sundews and thistles, which he had discarded at the bend in the river — had evolved into superweeds. Growing to a height that would have frightened any farmer, they had also flowered much earlier than they should have. It was almost as if they knew they were in a race against time and must flower before they were destroyed.

Fortunately for the man in the white coat, the super-weeds were growing in an area of poor land that no one wanted and few frequented.

Unaware that the weeds were growing out of control, the man in the white coat had turned his mind to something else. Some years previously, he had worked on a project that would have enabled cows to produce more twins and therefore increased their value. However, it had been less successful than he had hoped for, and so he had turned his attention to cloning. In these experiments he had bypassed nature's way of producing an animal — by mating. Instead, by using DNA from an adult — the very building-blocks of life — he had attempted to reprogramme a single egg cell in such a way that it would produce a clone or copy of the adult.

Spurred on by the announcement that scientists elsewhere had succeeded in cloning Dolly the sheep, he had pushed ahead with his own cloning programme, even though his work in this area had also been dogged by mistakes. With the help of people from a travelling circus, who had supplied him with the birds and animals he required, he had attempted to clone an ostrich, a llama, a pig, and a sheep. However, his methods had been seriously flawed from the start, and the clones that had been born were less than perfect copies. The ostrich clone had two necks and two heads, the llama a head at each end, the pig two faces, and the sheep a horn where it should have had a tail. In other experiments, his gene machine had got some of the genes mixed up, with the result that it had produced crosses between a fox and a cat, a peacock and a rooster.

Not to be deterred, the errant scientist had kept his creations. When they were big enough to be separated from their mothers, he had put them into a large, open enclosure where he continued to observe them. Soon he would sell them to the circus, where they would be paraded in front of people as freaks, not as the products of man's interference in nature. They would command a good price, he reckoned, and he badly needed the money, as he had been promised a grant for his research but had never received it. The promise had been made by a local politician, who had assured the scientist many times that he had made the necessary representations and that the grant had been approved. It was only when the money had failed to materialise that he realised he had been told a lot of lies.

As a mark of his dislike for the politician, who seemed to be able to lie out of both sides of his mouth at the same time, the scientist had named the two-headed ostrich a Liesalot. And because the two-headed llama seemed to be in a constant dilemma, never able to make up its mind which way to go or what to do, he called it a Dillylama. The sheep with a horn where it should have had a tail, he called a Ewe-ni-horn; the pig with two faces, a Gaze-pig.

It had been a rare type of pig that the man had tried to clone. To his surprise, he had found that the circus people had what was known in times past as a grey-hound pig. This breed of pig was common in the eighteenth and early nineteenth centuries. Unlike an ordinary pig, the greyhound pig had a long snout, two upward-curving tusks and two wattles, fleshy bow-shaped appendages, hanging from its neck. But most remarkable of all was its agility, for it was claimed that it could easily jump a five-barred gate. It was valued for the quality of its meat, but was very slow-growing.

The greyhound pig survived into this century, but in small numbers, and the last recorded sighting of one was in Liverpool during the Second World War. How the circus had come to have one, the scientist had no idea. And if it had ever been able to jump a five-barred gate, it was too old to do so now. But a younger pig, a clone, would be a great attraction. All his experiments had been able to produce, however, was a pig with two faces. Because of this, and the fact that greyhounds were once known as gazehounds, he had called it a Gaze-pig.

As for the cross between a peacock and a rooster, it was a very strange bird. It had all the characteristics of a peacock, except that it lacked the peacock's brilliant colours and had the less-exotic colours of a rooster. But, as if to make up for that loss, the gene machine had endowed it with a characteristic never before seen in this part of the world. To his great surprise, the man had seen it land, shake its tail and then, like a chameleon, take on the colours of its background so that it seemed to disappear. For this reason, and because it was neither one thing nor the other, he had called it a Cock-a-doodle-sham-cock.

Strange as that creature might seem, the man considered his greatest achievement to be the creation of an animal that was half-fox, half-cat, as such a cross was thought to be impossible. Some people might find this surprising, as there are many things about the fox — such as its way of pouncing — that are very like a cat. But the fact is, the fox is a member of the dog family, and despite the fact that country folk sometimes tell of seeing animals that are half-fox, half-dog, scientists say that even a cross between a fox and a dog is impossible.

In all probability, the man at the big house would once have agreed; but even he had not foreseen what the gene machine could do. As with the peacock and the rooster, the machine had got things mixed up, with the result that it had produced something which, he knew, would confound scientists the world over. He could also see that he had created, albeit by mistake, a hunter which would be without equal in the Irish countryside, combining as it did the physical attributes of two of nature's most expert predators. It had the nose and body of a fox, but the eyes and ears of a cat, and it was only when he saw it swish its long, sloping tail that he felt that perhaps the feline genes had gained the upper hand.

In any event, the man had decided to call his new creation a Fo-paw. The name was a play on the words 'four paws' and the French *'faux pas'*, which he took to mean 'a mistake'. Had he consulted his dictionary, he would have found that a *faux pas* is an embarrassing blunder — but he didn't feel the slightest bit embarrassed. He knew he had achieved something no other scientist had achieved. So he had also put the Fo-paw in the pen, intending to keep it there until he decided how to make money out of it. Unlike his other creations, however, the Fo-paw was not to be kept in captivity. Its instinct to hunt was too great, and, by some means known only to itself, it had escaped.

From remains the man had found in the woods, he knew the Fo-paw was feeding on wild rabbits and anything else it could find, but, despite all his efforts, he had failed to recapture it. Perhaps, he thought, he might call in some of his friends from the circus to help him. In the meantime, he was considering producing another hybrid — with the help of two fox cubs he had cornered in one of the sheds.

∾

The blue skies had given way to a cover of cloud, and the bright sunshine to a clamminess that suggested the cloud was laden with thunder as well as rain. It wasn't the best weather in which to hunt, as there was little wind and less scent, but the three foxes that now made their way towards the big house had other things on their minds besides hunting. Other creatures, they hoped, would soon find the clamminess more to their liking and perform one of nature's miracles, which might help free the cubs.

Having seen no sign of the howling dogs on her previous visit, Sinnéad had overcome her fears and agreed to go back to the big house, with She-la and Vickey, in an attempt to carry out the rescue. The plan had been devised by Old Sage Brush, and when the vixens had proposed that they should carry it out, their mates had objected. It was, the dogs had suggested, a job for them. But then, when they had thought about it, they had realised the vixens were right. The two dog foxes were needed to guard Old Sage Brush and Hop-along against a predator which they could not see, but which, they sensed, had not gone away.

As the vixens approached the big house, thoughts of the day she had been chased there by the howling dogs came flooding back into Sinnéad's mind. For a moment the memory, and the fears it held, threatened to make her turn back, but somehow she managed to push it to the back of her mind and keep going. From what Black Tip and Skulking Dog had said, she knew that the sounds coming from the field beyond the wood were not those of the howling dogs, but those of the strange creatures man kept in a pen.

At the edge of the wood, the vixens settled down in the cover of some scrub, beside what the dog foxes had called 'the Path of the Ants'. They knew, from what the dogs had told them, that the path ran from the house down towards the pen. There was no sign of the man in the white coat, and no scent on the path to suggest that it had been used recently by anything other than the ants, so She-la made her way back through the trees to the house.

Looking up at one of the windows, she could see that the man in the white coat was busy inside, and she quickly informed the others. The way was now clear for their next move.

Leaving She-la and Sinnéad to watch the path for any sign of danger, Vickey made her way down through the wood until she was opposite the pen. She was still a good distance away, but she could see that the creatures inside were exactly as Black Tip and Skulking Dog — and, indeed, Hop-along — had described them. Raising her head, she uttered a high-pitched screech, then lay down and waited.

The man in the big house came to the window and looked out, but, seeing nothing, returned to his test-tubes. He knew that in times past such an unearthly sound had put fear in the hearts of country people. In their ignorance, they had believed that it was the cry of a creature they called a banshee, and that it foretold a death. More enlightened people, however, knew it for what it was — the cry of a vixen.

Hearing the call, several of the creatures which the man in the white coat had created looked up, wide-eyed and curious. Then they looked at the tree in the middle of their pen, as an answering call came from one of the fox cubs. Out in the woods, Vickey smiled. The cubs, she knew, had recognised her call and would be ready for whatever happened next.

As the morning passed, the weather became even more warm and humid, and Vickey hoped they would be able to put their plan into action before it rained. Hurrying back to their hiding-place beside the path, she was informed by the others that the man appeared to be getting ready to feed the creatures in the pen. Vickey cocked her ears and, hearing him close a door up at the house, nodded.

'And what about the ants?' she asked, scanning the path. 'Are they ready yet?'

'Just about,' She-la told her.

'They're running all over the place,' said Sinnéad. 'I'd say it won't be long.'

As well as the smaller ants, which were coming and going from the holes in the path at an increasingly fast pace, a number of bigger, blacker ones were now wandering farther afield. Suddenly Sinnéad, who was lying with her eyes fixed on one of the holes, exclaimed, 'There's one! Look! And another!'

Vickey and She-la smiled. They could see other types of ants emerging from the hole. They were much bigger than the ones that seemed to be doing all the running around. Furthermore, they had sprouted wings, and as soon as they emerged they broke into flight. Before long, the air seemed to be full of flying ants, as the humidity triggered their aerial mating dance.

All along the path, ants from other underground

nests were taking to the air. At the same time, pairs that had mated earlier began dropping to the ground, and the foxes could feel them squirming on their fur. Some of the ants were also becoming entangled in the hair of the man with the white coat, who was now carrying buckets of food down to the pen. Stopping, the man put the buckets down and attempted to brush the ants away. They were, the foxes could see, crawling all over his white coat as they searched for whatever nature had planned for them.

'Come on,' whispered Vickey, and the other two followed her down through the shrubbery until they were almost opposite the gate of the pen. A few minutes later, the man arrived at the gate. Putting down the buckets once more, he took another swipe at the ants that were flying around his head.

Inside the pen, his weird creations were reacting in various ways. The Liesalot had just been joined by the Cock-a-doodle-sham-cock, and both were running around snapping up as many ants as they could. The Dillylama, in typical fashion, was prancing around in circles, the large brown eyes in each of its heads bulging in panic, neither head able to make up its mind what to do or where to go. Only the Gaze-pig and the Ewe-ni-horn appeared oblivious to the ants and were waiting patiently for the man to feed them.

By now the ants had become as numerous as a swarm of bees, or so it seemed to the vixens who watched from the cover of the shrubbery. To add to the confusion, birds of various descriptions, including wagtails and magpies, were swooping in and out among the nuptial flights. With considerably more experience of flight than the ants, they were plucking the newcomers from the air and filling their beaks for themselves and their young.

Flustered by the feeling that he was being dive-bombed by both the ants and the birds, the man in the white coat began running around in circles, brushing away his small tormentors with both hands, and shushing the birds, in an effort to rid himself of the plague that had descended upon him. To make matters worse, a fox was now running around his legs, and he feared he was going to trip over it at any moment.

Seeing that Sinnéad had succeeded in adding to the man's confusion, Vickey and She-la seized their chance and dashed through the open gate. The strange occupants of the pen scattered before them, and, running over to the tree in the middle, they called to the cubs to come down. After what seemed an eternity, Firefly gingerly descended from the upper branches and joined them.

'Where's Blaze?' cried She-la, looking up into the tree.

'Man took her,' Firefly panted. 'He has her in the big house.'

'Come on,' said Vickey, 'before he closes the gate. Hurry!'

As the foxes sped towards the gate, the man saw them drive his beloved creations before them. He had barely time to step out of the way before the Liesalot collided with the partly open gate and sent it crashing outwards. The Dillylama, having been unable to make up its own mind, took off after it, and all his efforts to stop it failed. The fox that had been running around his legs had gone, but he was almost knocked off his feet by the Gaze-pig and the Ewe-ni-horn. Then the Cock-a-doodle-sham-cock uttered a shriek and a 'cock-a-doodle-do' and sailed past him, towards the trees. There it strutted around at the edge of the under-growth, opened out its large fan-shaped tail and, with a wiggle, disappeared.

The small birds that had been feeding on the ants had flown off when the creatures had rushed from the pen, and now that the stampede was over, they returned. Taking to his heels, the man covered his head with his hands and ran back up the path. The yard, it seemed, was also full of flying ants, so he rushed into the house and slammed the door behind him.

But if it was refuge he was seeking, he soon found that he had another intruder. The door was old and warped, and, seeing it bounce open again, She-la dashed in after him.

From the cover of the trees, Vickey, Sinnéad and little Firefly watched and waited with bated breath. No sooner had She-la gone into the house than they heard the man shouting and the sound of breaking glass. She-la, they knew, was risking her life in a desperate bid to rescue Blaze, but what was happening inside they couldn't imagine. This was not in Old Sage Brush's plan, and instinct told them that even a plague of flies would not be able to help her.

Beyond the door, She-la found herself in a room full of broad tables and high stools. The tables were littered with glasses of all shapes and sizes, and these contained liquids of every colour. But it's doubtful if she was even aware of these as she dashed around the man's legs and the stools. All she was aware of was the dreadful stench of the man-made liquids and the smell of fear.

The man, who was still trying to pull the ants from his hair, was startled to see a fox running past him. He immediately made a lunge at it, but he missed, smashing some of the glasses on the table with his elbow and overturning others. By the time he had righted the unbroken glasses, he saw that the fox had run around the table and was perched on one of the stools on the far side. Rushing around after it, he lunged at it again. This time it dashed across the table, toppling a rack of test-tubes and breaking them into smithereens.

Appalled by the destruction, the man reached out to try and save as many of his precious liquids as he could. The fox was only of secondary importance, he told himself, and if he continued to pursue it there was no telling what damage it would do. It hadn't occurred to him that the fox might have been attracted to his laboratory by the cub he had in a cage in the corner. So concerned was he with saving his various concoctions that he didn't even see the intruder clawing at the cage. And when he did, it was too late.

Frightened as she was by the sound of breaking glass, Blaze was overjoyed to see She-la, and both of them began pulling and pushing in a desperate attempt to force open the door of the cage. Fortunately, the door was only held in place by a metal staple, and when this was dislodged it swung open. Before the man realised what was happening, the two foxes were racing towards the door and he was left in the debris of his damaged laboratory, with neither plant nor clone to show for all his hard work.

7

The Forbidden Word

Blaze and Firefly rushed into the earth beneath the blackthorns to inform Hop-along that the tall bird was eating stones. Before he could ask them any questions, they were gone again, so he hobbled out to see what they were talking about. To his amazement, he saw the tall bird with the two heads standing nearby. It had found a place where the soil was bare, and while one head was nibbling at the hedge above it, the other was picking up all the pebbles it could find. Both its beaks, he could see, were almost full, and when they could hold no more, they began to swallow, each mouthful making a large bulge in each neck as it moved slowly down towards the body.

Hop-along could not know that, because the big bird had no teeth for chewing its food, it was picking up pebbles the way a hen would pick up grit, to help grind its food into a more digestible pulp. But what surprised him more was that the bird should be so near his home.

Then, as he looked around, he was startled to find that most of the other creatures that had escaped from the big house were there as well. The animal which he thought was a two-headed deer was grazing nearby, its two heads raised, their big brown eyes watching his every move. The sheep with a horn where it should have had a tail was nibbling grass, while the two-faced pig was snuffling around for whatever food it could find beneath the grass.

As he tried to take in the enormity of what was happening, Hop-along saw that, even though the pig was quite a young animal, it had overturned sod after sod with its noses, so that a large patch of the field outside his earth looked as if it had been churned up by one of man's machines. Hobbling over as fast as his three legs could carry him, he demanded to know what the pig thought it was doing.

Taken aback, the pig replied, 'Nothing.'

'What do you mean, nothing?' asked Hop-along. 'Why are you digging up the field? And what are all these — these ....' He searched for a word that would describe the other creatures, but, finding none, added, 'What are all these doing here?'

The pig looked at Hop-along with one of its faces and told him, 'When our friends — your friends — released us from the pen, we followed them here. Why, did we do wrong?'

'But — but you can't stay here,' exclaimed Hop-along. 'And what are you doing, digging up the field?'

'I'm just searching for something to eat,' the pig replied. 'You know, like slugs and worms and roots. That sort of thing. The others are just nibbling the grass. And why can't we stay here? I mean, where else can we go? Where else would we stay but with our friends who released us?'

Hop-along was about to tell the pig that, from what he had heard, they had really escaped by accident, but somehow he felt sorry for it, so he just said, 'But you can't stay here. Not beside our earth. If man comes looking for you, he'll find us as well, and if that happens, he'll kill us.'

On hearing that, the pig lay down and began to sob. 'We have no one else to turn to,' he sobbed. 'No mothers, no fathers, no families — nothing.'

Mesmerised by what was happening, the cubs had remained silent, but on hearing this, Blaze said, 'How can that be? Everybody has a mother and a father. We all have a family.'

The pig sniffed to hold back its tears. 'Not us,' it replied. 'Not now. But some of us remember that once we did have mothers. At least, I do. I seem to remember two mothers. Maybe three.' Hop-along couldn't know that the pig was remembering not only the mother that had given birth to him, but the other adults that had been used in the cloning process. He was about to say that no one could have two mothers, when the pig continued, 'One had a big family. In my mind's eye I can see all my brothers and sisters suckling at her teats. But then they were all taken away. I think man killed them and ate them.'

Appalled, Firefly asked, 'But how do you know this? I mean, if you weren't there?'

'How do you know I wasn't there?' asked the pig.

'Well,' said Firefly, 'I mean, if you were there, you

would have been eaten too, wouldn't you?'

The pig sniffed again, saying, 'I suppose so.'

'So how do you know all this?' asked Hop-along.

'I don't know,' the pig admitted, 'but I do.'

'Well, you can't stay here,' Hop-along told it, 'or we're the ones who'll be killed.'

'Why, does man eat you too?' asked the pig.

Hop-along shook his head. 'No. He hunts us for our fur and he hunts us for fun. But he doesn't eat us.'

'Perhaps,' suggested the pig, 'it might be safer for all of us if we hid in the woods.'

'Good idea,' said Hop-along. 'But when man sees the way you've dug up the grass, he'll know you've been here.'

It was then Hop-along realised that he was talking to quite an intelligent animal, for, having pondered this for a moment, the pig said, 'The cows. Perhaps man will think the cows have done it.'

The eyes of the fox cubs lit up, and Blaze said, 'That's a great idea. But how are we going to get the cows to come here? I mean, they won't move for us the way they move for dogs.'

'My memory tells me that cows are curious creatures,' replied the pig. 'And my other face shows me that they are already on their way.'

The pig was right. And even after Hop-along's visitors had disappeared into the woods, the cows milled around the blackthorns, curious about what kind of creatures had been there, but not intelligent enough to know why they had gone.

It was now painfully obvious to Hop-along that, in his fanciful flight with the wind, he had caused a problem for himself and his friends. He had begun a sequence of events that had drawn these strange creatures upon them, and he knew it would only be a matter of time before man followed. That being so, he knew that the sooner the other foxes were alerted, the better.

When their cubs had returned safely, Scat and Flame had been overjoyed, but their joy had quickly turned to anger and they had rebuked the two cubs for not doing what they had been told. Anger had then given way to annoyance, and annoyance had finally subsided with the realisation that the cubs had got such a fright that they were unlikely to disobey their elders again. After that, Scat had taken Flame up to the evergreens, and there he would look after her until she recovered from the ordeal of suckling such boisterous young.

She-la, who had gone part of the way with Scat and Flame, had caught a rabbit, and now, as she brought it back to the earth, she wondered what all the cows were doing, nosing around the blackthorns. The smell of the cows and their droppings had obliterated any other scent she might have picked up, and she was shocked to learn from Hop-along and the excited cubs that the creatures from the big house had followed them.

'Have you alerted the others?' she asked.

Hop-along shook his head. 'We were waiting for the cows to go. And for you to come back.' He snapped at the cubs, who were tearing frantically at the rabbit, and told them to wait their turn.

'All right,' said She-la, 'when you finish eating, take Blaze and Firefly and go up and tell Old Sage Brush what has happened. I'll go over to the old quarry and see if I can find Black Tip and Vickey.'

By the time Hop-along had eaten his fill, and the cubs had devoured what was left of the rabbit, they found that the cows had wandered away from their earth and were grazing in another part of the field. Hop-along was relieved to see that the ground had been so mulched up by the cows' feet, no trace remained of the creatures from the big house, and he wondered again at the fact that the pig had come up with such a good idea.

'As soon as I let Vickey and Black Tip know what has happened,' said She-la, 'I'll follow you.'

Hop-along hobbled off towards the woods with the two cubs. Not far inside, they spotted the creatures from the big house resting in the shade, and, afraid that they might follow them, they slipped quietly past. Whether it was because of the presence of such creatures, Hop-along didn't know, but the woods were quieter than usual. The small birds, he could see, were flitting about in the trees, but they weren't singing.

He was about to say something to the cubs when there was an ear-piercing screech and a loud 'cock-a-doodle-do'. A moment later, the rainbow bird with the head of a cock came gliding down from the trees and, on landing, fanned out its tail. Annoyed that it had betrayed their presence, Hop-along hobbled towards it as fast as he could, only to see it wiggle its tail and disappear. Forgetting for a moment that the cubs were with him, he exclaimed, 'That flithengibber has got to go.'

The cubs stopped and looked at each other, shocked that their grand-dog should use the forbidden word. From the time they had opened their eyes and learned to speak, they had been warned never to say 'flithen-gibber'. It was, the cubs had been told, an exclamation that a fox out hunting on its own might use if it was spotted by a blackbird or a magpie. Such a bird loved to tell the whole world, with its loud chattering or gibbering and its flashy, flittering movements, that there was a fox on the prowl. If the fox was taken by surprise and got a fright, it would curse its tormentor, calling it a flithengibber. However, the word was forbidden in normal conversation, as no fox would admit that it had been surprised by a bird, let alone frightened by one.

'Gibbering' means the same to man as it does to the fox, but the meaning of 'flithen' might be less obvious. Man might hear in it slight resonances of the words 'flight' and 'flitter'. He might even see in it some of the letters of the word 'frighten'. However, the cubs knew it meant much more than that. F, their mother had told them, showed that it was a *fox* word, a curse on the birds with the flicking tails that dared to betray a fox's presence. L was for 'loud-mouth', and for looking at the bird with all the *loathing* the fox could muster. I was for 'insult', meaning that the word was meant to insult the bird as much as possible. T was to *tell* the bird to fly off and mind its own business. H was to *hope* that the bird would be consigned to the afterlife — not to the happy hunting-ground where it could fly free of danger and disease, but to a bottomless pit, never to fly again. E was for the fox's intention to make its *exit* whenever it could, leaving the bird with the raucous beak to throw its evil eye on something else. N meant *never* to tell any other fox what had happened, and *never* to be caught unawares again.

Little wonder, then, that the cubs were shocked to hear the forbidden word — so shocked, in fact, that with one accord they turned and ran back towards the blackthorns to tell She-la.

Hop-along turned and was about to call the cubs back when he realised he would be wasting his time, so he just smiled and kept going. A short time later he arrived at the oak tree where Old Sage Brush lived, and was delighted to find that Skulking Dog and Sinnéad were also there. As he settled down, he saw that the others had brought the old fox some food, and he was wondering how he was going to break the news about their unexpected visitors when Old Sage Brush said, 'Well, Hop-along, what brings you here?'

Skulking Dog smiled at Sinnéad. 'Maybe he's been seeing things again.'

'You wouldn't smile if you'd seen what I've just seen,' said Hop-along.

'And what would that be?' asked the old fox.

'The creatures from the big house,' Hop-along told him. 'They're in the woods.'

Skulking Dog sprang to his feet. He was no longer smiling, and he demanded, 'Where? You mean, in these woods?'

Hop-along nodded and told them how he had come out of the blackthorns to find that the creatures had followed them from the big house. 'The pig says you're his friends,' added Hop-along, looking at Sinnéad. 'That you helped them escape.'

Before Sinnéad could protest that the creatures had got out of the enclosure by accident, Old Sage Brush said to Hop-along, 'That's something I meant to ask you. You told me that the first time you saw these creatures, they talked to you. Even the big bird.'

'That's right,' Hop-along told him. 'And I talked to them.'

'But how can that be?' asked Sinnéad. 'I mean, we can talk to the other animals that live in the Land of Sinna. But these creatures — we've never seen them before.'

'I don't know,' replied Hop-along. 'But they do talk. The big bird speaks with both beaks and says different things, almost as if each head is of a different mind. And the pig with two faces — maybe it has two minds as well as two faces, but they must be two minds working as one, for it's very intelligent.'

Just then, Black Tip and Vickey arrived, closely followed by She-la and the cubs.

'Hop-along used the forbidden word,' Blaze told Old Sage Brush.

'That's right,' said Firefly. 'I heard him too.'

Hop-along was about to say something when there was another harsh screech and a loud 'cock-a-doodle-do'. Not knowing what was happening, but sensing danger, Old Sage Brush immediately retreated to his earth, and the others scurried in after him. Looking out, She-la saw the half-cock-half-rainbow-bird gliding down from the branches of a nearby tree. Then, almost as if it had guided its friends to the spot, the other creatures from the big house emerged from the trees and gathered around the ancient oak.

'Hop-along's right,' She-la whispered. 'That flithen-gibber *will* have to go.'

This time the cubs expressed no shock at hearing the forbidden word. Their eyes were transfixed by the movements of the other bird, whose two long necks were sweeping down so that the four big eyes in its two bald heads could look in at the foxes that had squeezed in under the gnarled roots.

Now, for the first time, the adult foxes knew how the cubs must have felt when they were closed in with the creatures at the big house. Sinnéad was particularly concerned about her father. Being feeble and blind, he would not be able to make a run for it. Similar thoughts were going through She-la's mind as she wondered how Hop-along was going to get away. They were all crouching, afraid that the tall bird might try and pluck one of them out, when, to their surprise, the creatures turned around and went away.

Relieved, but curious, Black Tip and Skulking Dog ventured out, closely followed by the vixens. Hearing them gasp, Old Sage Brush and Hop-along asked if the creatures had gone. 'No,' Sinnéad called back to them. 'At least, not very far. But don't worry. They're with Ratwiddle!'

Old Sage Brush and Hop-along emerged from the earth, and the old fox found himself trying to imagine the scene that the others described. In a clearing a short distance away, Ratwiddle was lying with his nose in the air, and all the creatures, big and small, had settled around him. Now and then the animal which they took to be a two-headed deer would utter a high-pitched moan, and the others would nod, almost as if they were somehow in communication with one another and with Ratwiddle. Yet the other foxes knew that no one, not even themselves, could communicate with Ratwiddle, who seemed to live in a world of his own.

Without warning, Ratwiddle got up and ran off through the woods. Seeing the creatures getting to their feet, the vixens were getting ready to lead Old Sage Brush and Hop-along in the opposite direction when, to their amazement, the two-faced pig took off after Ratwiddle. After some hesitation, the sheep with a horn where it should have had a tail took off after the pig. For a moment the tall bird strutted around like a turkeycock, shuffling its short, brown-feathered wings. At the same time, one head looked one way and the other head looked the other, almost as if it was telling itself to go in different directions. Then its long, bony legs sprang into action and it raced off after the sheep. By this time, the two-headed deer was prancing around in circles, apparently unable to make up its mind what to do. Finally it hopped sideways across the clearing, spun around and took off after the big bird.

Sinnéad, who had been trying to describe it all to her father, sighed with relief. 'I wonder where they've gone.'

'It doesn't matter,' said She-la. 'They're gone, and that's the important thing.'

Suddenly there was a piercing screech, followed by a loud 'cock-a-doodle-do', and Skulking Dog exclaimed, 'They're not all gone.' Even as he spoke, the rainbow bird with the cock's head came gliding into the clearing again and began pecking around for food.

'Do you know, I think it's keeping an eye on us,' said Black Tip.

Hop-along nodded. 'And it'll tell the others where we are.'

'Not only that,' said Old Sage Brush. 'It'll also tell man.' He made his way slowly back to his earth beneath the tree, and as the others settled in around him, he added, 'We'll have to figure out some way to get rid of it.'

'Maybe we can catch it,' suggested She-la, who was worried that the bird with the raucous call might expose them to another hunter — the fox-cat.

Having decided that the best way to catch the bird was to surround it, several of the foxes spread out and crept quietly through the undergrowth. From the entrance to the earth, Hop-along and the cubs watched and waited. The bird, they could see, was pecking away at the ground, apparently unaware that it was being surrounded.

It wasn't long, however, before the hunters discovered that they were dealing with no ordinary bird. Sometimes it would just shiver its fan-shaped tail and disappear, only to re-emerge a short distance away. And when did they get what seemed a good opportunity to pounce on it, it would just take to the air and crow at them from a branch of the nearest tree.

Returning to the earth, She-la was sorely tempted to use the forbidden word again, but, mindful of the fact that the cubs were present and not wishing to set them a bad example, she lay down outside and looked up at the creature that was crowing at their inability to catch it.

Suddenly, Skulking Dog, who was also lying watching the bird, got up, saying, 'I've an idea.'

Curious to know what it was, the others gathered around, and when Black Tip heard that it would involve a visit to another farmyard, he said, 'It would be dangerous. But, you know, it might just work. I'll go with you.'

'No,' said Sinnéad. 'I'll go.'

Black Tip nodded. Skulking Dog, he knew, had been very fond of raiding hen-pens, and had almost been killed before Old Sage Brush had shown him that there were safer ways to forage for food. Sinnéad, being his mate, would want to keep an eye on him, just in case he might be tempted to return to his old ways.

Not far beyond the woods, the foxes knew, was a farm where the hens were still allowed to range free. Occasionally a passing fox might snatch a hen, but those who had an earth in the area preferred to go farther afield for their supper, as the last thing they wanted was to draw the farmer down upon them. Now, Skulking Dog was planning to take several of the hens — and, if his plan worked, to put them back again!

There was a time, as Black Tip had remembered, when Skulking Dog would have got so excited by the presence of hens that he would have run among them snapping the head off each and every one. If he had been lucky, he would have escaped with only a single bird — or, more likely, with the farmer's shotgun pellets in his rump. Thanks to Old Sage Brush, he was now more cautious. But in those raids on the farms, he had learned that hens, like rabbits, had a peculiar weakness. The fright of being caught by a fox would make them go into a dead faint. Then, a few minutes later, they would come to life again.

And so he and his mate stalked the hens in a small field at the back of the farmyard, and, in the same way that the cubs had been taught to pull a worm from the ground without breaking it, they caught two hens around the neck without killing them. As soon as they felt the hens going limp, they knew they were in a dead faint, and, catching them gently around the wings, they carried them up to the woods.

When Skulking Dog and Sinnéad arrived back at the oak tree, the other foxes told them that the troublesome bird was still perched on a high branch, watching them. They immediately left the two hens in the clearing and retreated to the surrounding shrubbery to see what would happen. Slowly, the two hens stirred back to life, rose to their feet and wandered around as if they were in a daze.

Skulking Dog looked at Sinnéad and then up at the treetops. Which part of the bird in the tree had the strongest instinct, he wondered — the head or the body? A moment later, his question was answered. There was a screech and a 'cock-a-doodle-do', and the big bird swooped down to land beside the hens.

Skulking Dog smiled. His hunch had been right. The bird was being ruled by its head, and its head was that of a rooster. As it fanned out its tail and wiggled it in a mating dance, the hens uttered screeches of their own, flapped into flight and headed back towards the farm. Their would-be suitor ran after them, and the foxes followed, making sure that the big bird didn't lose sight of the hens or of his ardour for the opposite sex.

Soon the hens were back in the farmyard, and when

the foxes arrived they heard a screech and a 'cock-a-doodle-do'. Looking up, they saw the other bird standing on the gable-end of an outbuilding. Being neither one thing nor the other, this strange creature, they reckoned, would not be able to mate with the hens. In all probability, its interest in them was all in its mind. Nevertheless, the sight of the hens would, hopefully, keep it happy and give it something else to crow about besides the foxes in the wood.

8

The Fox and the Ewe-ni-horn

There was now another strange collection of animals at the big house. Not as strange, perhaps, as the creatures that had escaped from the pen, but strange nevertheless. There were brown-and-white horses, which people called piebalds but which in reality were skewbalds, and there were black-and-white horses, which people called skewbalds but which in reality were piebalds. There were also white horses and black horses, and golden palominos with fine flowing manes and lovely long tails.

Then there were the dogs. There were big dogs and small dogs, some with very long legs, some with very short legs, some with long hair, some with short hair, some with straight tails, some with curly tails and some with hardly any tails at all. There were purebreds and mongrels, some white, some black, some grey, some brown, some with all these colours, and a couple of smaller ones with an odd-looking black patch over one eye. There were also some fancy-looking dogs, with delicate legs and delicate manners, and haircuts that would have been better suited to the people who were with them.

The people themselves were also a strange collection. There were tall people and small people, thin people and fat people, people with horses and people without horses, people with dogs and people without dogs, people in riding gear and people in costumes, people with broad-brimmed hats and people with scarves tied around their heads. And they were all gathered around the man in the white coat.

After some discussion — and it was difficult, with so many people trying to talk at the same time — a decision was taken to go in a particular direction, for the man in the white coat had seen his creatures run towards Glensinna — or, as it was known in Gaelic, *Gleann an tSionnaigh Bháin*, the Valley of the White Fox. All the people with horses mounted up and cantered off, and all the people with dogs followed on foot — all, that is, except the people with the dogs with fancy haircuts. These were two women who were grossly overweight, and it was with great reluctance that they released their dogs so that they could go too.

As the man in the white coat watched the circus people go in search of his creations, he had mixed feelings. On the one hand, he needed the money they had promised to pay him for what they considered to be freaks. On the other, he would have liked to keep his creations under observation for longer, for there were some things about them he had not told the circus people ....

The Liesalot had been cloned from an old ostrich, and the man had observed that for some reason it was ageing faster than it should have, while the Dillylama had two heads but only one heart. As a result, he feared that they might not survive too long, especially if they were hunted too hard. The Ewe-ni-horn might prove to be a big attraction in a circus, but it was as stubborn as a goat and he could not imagine that it could be trained. And while pigs were also considered to be animals that could not be trained, the Gaze-pig not only had two faces, it had two brains and was, he had found, the most intelligent of them all.

Even the man who had created these strange birds and animals, however, was unaware that they had other characteristics that were unique — characteristics that would have made them much more valuable to science than to a circus. He saw them only as mistakes. And, as he turned to go back into the big house, he was already turning his mind to another mistake. The circus people had told him that some of the experimental plants he had discarded down at the bend in the river had taken root, and he realised he would have to concoct an especially strong spray to kill them.

~

It was with great curiosity that the birds in the bushes looked down at their unusual visitors, but even the magpies, which are more inquisitive than other birds, kept their distance.

From the safety of the upper branches, a blue tit, its

beak full of green caterpillars, paused to look at the long-legged bird with two necks in the quarry below. It had also stuffed its beaks, but not with caterpillars. It had been nibbling and plucking at anything it could find. And, while the blue tit would take its mouthful back to its young, the big bird had swallowed each mouthful as one ball, and the blue tit watched in wonder as the balls slowly slipped down each long neck. Before flying off to its nest, the blue tit wondered if the big bird could fly and where it would build its nest, but it was only a fleeting thought. The blue tit was small, and so was its brain; it wasn't capable of any deep thoughts on the matter, and it soon forgot about it.

The foxes were not so fortunate. As long as these strange creatures remained with them, so too would the danger that man might come looking for them. The problem was even more acute for Black Tip and Vickey, as their earth was in the quarry. They had returned to find that Ratwiddle had made his way there, and that the creatures had followed him. Out of sight of man, they were moving around under the bushes, poking and nibbling at anything they could find.

Realising that they could not use their earth while the creatures were in the quarry, Black Tip and Vickey made their way back up to the oak tree and informed Old Sage Brush of what had happened.

'I don't know what Ratwiddle thinks he's doing,' declared Vickey. 'I mean, he knows we live in the quarry, and we wouldn't get any peace, especially with that big bird pecking in at us.'

'Anyway,' said Black Tip, 'it would be too dangerous for us to stay there now. If man comes looking for them, he would find us too.'

Old Sage Brush nodded. 'It's difficult to know what's

in Ratwiddle's mind, or if there's anything in it at all. But, you know, it's an ideal place for those creatures to hide. Nobody will see them.'

'But they'll have to come out to eat,' said Black Tip. 'There's not much for them in there.'

Once again the old fox nodded. 'Unless,' he said, 'we could persuade them to stay in there during the day and come out to eat at night.'

'But —' protested Vickey.

'I know, I know,' said Old Sage Brush. 'But just for a while ... until we think of somewhere else to hide them.'

Black Tip shook his head. 'That's not going to be easy. I mean, it's not as if they're small or look like anything else.'

'The pig looks like a pig, and the sheep looks like a sheep,' said the old fox. 'Isn't that right?'

'Well, more or less,' grunted Black Tip. 'But the other two — I don't know what they look like.'

'I'll tell you what you can do,' said Old Sage Brush. 'Hop-along says the pig is very intelligent. Why don't you ask it to come up and see me? Maybe we can work something out.'

Black Tip and Vickey exchanged a look which reflected their frustration, but, unable to suggest anything better, they agreed to do as the old fox asked, and a short time later they returned with the pig.

'Are you sure the others haven't followed you?' asked Old Sage Brush, who was lying in the darkness of his earth beneath the tree.

Black Tip, who was lying outside with Vickey and the pig, was about to answer, when the pig said, 'No, they're still in the quarry. I told them to stay there until I returned.'

Old Sage Brush was amused to hear a pig talk in a

way he could understand. At the same time, he wasn't sure whether they were actually talking to each other, or exchanging thoughts.

What neither the fox nor the pig — nor, indeed, the man in the white coat — knew was that, by some quirk of the gene machine, his creations, by exercising a sort of telepathy, could communicate with one another and with other creatures in a way that man could not. And, because they had been cloned from adults, they were conscious of having had previous existences. They remembered other lives — and, in some cases, the deaths of what they believed were their mothers.

Strange as it may seem, they had also looked upon the man in the white coat as a mother-figure, and had even come to know the names he had allotted to them.

'Pig,' said Old Sage Brush.

'Gaze-pig,' said the pig. 'My name's Gaze-pig.' He paused. 'I know you cannot see me, but I have two faces. With one face I am watching you, and with my other face I am watching your friends.'

'How do you know I am blind?' asked the old fox.

The pig grunted. 'I don't know. I just know.'

Now Old Sage Brush was fairly sure they were exchanging thoughts rather than words, and he asked, 'How many eyes have you got?'

'Three,' the pig replied. 'One on each side and one in the middle.'

The old fox smiled. 'Well, now, Gaze-pig, that must give you a great advantage over everything else.'

The pig nodded. 'It does, all right. I can see what's in front and what's to the side at the same time.' He paused. 'And, just in case you're wondering, I have two ears and two noses.'

'Hmm,' mused Old Sage Brush, who was trying

to envisage it all. 'That must be a great advantage too. It certainly would be for a fox. Imagine being able to scent the wind with two noses! Tell me, how old are you?'

When the pig shook its two faces to indicate that it didn't know, Black Tip told the old fox, 'He's only a young pig — not fully grown.'

'And where did you come from?' asked Old Sage Brush.

'I don't know,' the pig replied. 'Sometimes I seem to see myself running like the wind across the fields, sailing over all the fences and gates I come to.'

Black Tip looked at Vickey and raised his eyes to the skies, as if to say, 'Where have we heard that before?' Instead, he told the pig, 'A friend of ours sometimes imagines the same thing.'

'And he has only three legs,' added Vickey.

'I know him,' said the pig. 'I mean, I met him.'

'I know you came from the big house,' Vickey went on, 'but Hop-along — he's the one with three legs — he said you remember having a mother.'

'Sometimes I remember having a mother,' the pig told her. 'Other times I see myself as my mother, and I seem to remember my mother's mother. It's all very strange. Maybe it's because I have two faces. I don't know.'

'And what about the others?' asked Old Sage Brush. 'Tell me about them.'

'Well, as you know, the Liesalot has two heads too ....' the pig began.

'The Liesalot?' asked Vickey. 'Which one is that?'

'The big bird. Man calls it a Liesalot. Why, I don't know. But you want to be careful about what it tells you.'

'Why?' asked Black Tip.

The pig, who was looking at Vickey with one eye

and Old Sage Brush with another, turned the third towards Black Tip and told him, 'Because it speaks with two minds. They never seem to speak as one, and the problem is, you can never tell which is telling the truth.'

Old Sage Brush nodded. 'So Hop-along was telling us. And that other animal — the one that looks like a deer with two heads?'

'Man calls it a Dillylama,' the pig informed him. 'Its two minds do seem to think as one, but even with two minds, it never seems to be able to make up its mind, if you know what I mean.'

The old fox took a deep breath, as if to indicate that he found the whole thing very perplexing. 'And the sheep, or whatever it is?'

The pig smiled with both faces and told him, 'That's a Ewe-ni-horn.'

'A what?' exclaimed Black Tip and Vickey at the same time.

'A Ewe-ni-horn,' repeated the pig. 'At least, that's what man calls it. You know, it's got a horn where ....'

'I know,' said Old Sage Brush. 'And where did it come from?'

'You mean the horn?'

The old fox laughed. 'No, the sheep.'

The pig shrugged. 'I don't know. The same place as the rest of us, I suppose — wherever that is. But you want to watch yourself when you're talking to it. It can be very stubborn, and if it gets you with that horn you'll be in trouble.'

'We're in trouble as it is,' said Black Tip.

'You mean, because of us?' asked the pig.

'Well, for a start,' Vickey told him, 'the quarry is where we live — or, at least, that's where we did live, until you and your friends took it over.'

'But Ratwiddle told us we would be safe there,' said the pig.

Black Tip and Vickey looked at each other again. In all their lives, they had never been able to converse in any sensible way with Ratwiddle, and yet he had been able to communicate with these creatures. The pig even knew his name!

Old Sage Brush came out and lay down beside the pig, a gesture which the other two knew meant he had taken a liking to their unusual visitor. 'The problem, Gaze-pig,' he said, 'is that you would have to stay in the quarry all day and only come out to eat at night. And I can't see some of your friends doing that.'

The pig nodded. 'I suppose you're right. What do you think we should do, then?'

'Well,' continued the old fox, 'that bird — the noisy one ....'

The pig turned to look at him with one of its eyes. 'You mean the Cock-a-doodle-sham-cock? Where did it go?'

'The Cock-a-doodle-what?' asked Black Tip.

'The Cock-a-doodle-sham-cock,' repeated the pig. 'You want to be careful of it. It's very noisy, and it can — well, disappear.'

Vickey nodded. 'We know. But Skulking Dog — he's one of our friends — he made it disappear, all right.'

The pig looked at the foxes with distress showing in both his faces. 'He didn't ... he didn't kill it, did he?'

Black Tip shook his head. 'No, he just encouraged it to go to a farm nearby. It's all right.'

'I think,' said Old Sage Brush, 'we should encourage the Ewe-ni-horn to do the same.'

'You mean,' said the pig, 'it should hide on a farm?'

'Why not?' replied the old fox. 'After all, who's going to notice one more sheep on a farm — even if it has a horn where it should have a tail?'

Black Tip and Vickey nodded and laughed, and the little pig, seeing the wisdom of the suggestion and the funny side of it at the same time, laughed heartily too. He also agreed to help them, and, without further delay, he went with Black Tip and Vickey to the quarry. There they found that his friends had nibbled and pecked at all they could find, and were now resting beneath the bushes.

Because the Ewe-ni-horn had been cloned from a sheep, it was distrustful of the foxes, and when Black Tip and Vickey got too near, it made this known to them in no uncertain manner. Flexing its long, pointed horn, it reversed rapidly, stabbing at them in the same way that a wasp would try to sting. Taken by surprise, Black Tip and Vickey hopped back to a safe distance and listened while the Gaze-pig tried to convince his friends that they would all have to find safer hiding-places.

'What better place for you to hide,' he told the Ewe-ni-horn, 'than in among a flock of sheep? And who better to show you the way than our friends who released us from the pen?'

The Ewe-ni-horn bleated and, as it settled itself once again, said, 'But I seem to have knowledge of foxes. Memories. I see my mother butting a fox with her head. I think it's lambing time. She's afraid it will take a lamb, especially if the lamb is weak. I see the fox running through our flock, and we scatter. We do not trust the fox.'

'But what have you to fear?' asked Black Tip. 'You're a strong sheep; and, as well as having horns on your head, you have a fine pointed horn to protect your rear. All we want to do is show you where the flock is, so you can hide in it.'

'If you stay here,' Vickey pointed out, 'you'll bring danger upon yourselves — and us.'

Seeing that the Ewe-ni-horn still wasn't convinced, the Gaze-pig said, 'What if the weakest of the foxes was to show you the way?'

'You mean the one with three legs?' asked the Ewe-ni-horn.

The Gaze-pig nodded. 'It wouldn't be a threat to you, would it?'

'I suppose not,' the Ewe-ni-horn conceded.

Vickey immediately dashed up to the blackthorns and informed Hop-along of the pig's proposal. She-la, anxious as always for her mate's safety, was firmly against it. Hop-along, on the other hand, was more anxious than any of them to have the creatures moved to another part of the valley. He assured She-la that he would be all right and, in spite of her objections, agreed to take the Ewe-ni-horn to the flock of sheep.

So it was that, a short time later, two creatures that had been disfigured by the works of man — a sheep with a horn where it should have had a tail, and a fox with a gap where it should have had a leg — made their way through the fields. The other foxes watched anxiously as they left. Now and then, they saw the Ewe-ni-horn take a reverse dash at Hop-along to make him keep his distance, and they wondered if they should have gone with him. However, they had agreed to let him go on his own; and, in any event, they wanted to make sure that the other creatures stayed in the quarry where they wouldn't be seen.

How much more they would have worried had they known that yet another creature was watching Hop-along go.

~

Sometimes, it seemed to Hop-along, the Ewe-ni-horn forgot what it was doing and where it was going, for now and then it would stop to nibble the grass. When he urged it to hurry, it would give a plaintive bleat and continue to nibble. Yet when he hobbled around behind it so as to encourage it to keep going, it would raise its pointed horn and take a run at him, reversing with such speed that he had to use all the strength in his three legs to hop out of the way. How, he wondered, was he ever going to get it to the field where the farmer kept his sheep?

Unknown to Hop-along, danger was now coming at them from two directions.

'It's the Fo-paw!' bleated the Ewe-ni-horn, and, with a burst of speed, it took off in a wide circle.

This was a name that Hop-along had not heard the Gaze-pig speak of, but when he turned to see what had frightened the Ewe-ni-horn, he found himself looking into a face that he had seen before. It had the nose of a fox, but the eyes and ears of a cat. Furthermore, he could see that its long, sweeping tail was wagging like a cat's tail, indicating that it was about to pounce!

Too late, Hop-along realised that he had forgotten about the fox-cat that had frightened him so much. For some reason, he had assumed that it would stay on the other side of the river. Now he was face to face with it once more.

Before he could move, it sprang, hitting him with the full weight of its body, bowling him over and over in a ferocious attack. At the same time, he felt its claws digging into him and its teeth — the sharp teeth of a fox — snapping and searching for a vital spot in his neck. In desperation, he snapped back and clawed, but it was no use, not with only one forepaw. He was unable to keep it away from him, and the creature's jaws closed on his throat. Powerless to stop it, he felt the life slowly being squeezed from his body.

Hop-along had almost resigned himself to the darkness which he knew was death when, suddenly, he felt the creature release its grip. Rolling over, he scrambled unsteadily to his feet and looked around.

To his amazement, he saw the Ewe-ni-horn reversing at great speed towards his attacker. Despite its agility, the creature was unable to get out of the way in time, and the horn caught it in the rump. With a squeal that was the cry of neither cat nor fox, it jumped into the air and, on landing, took off into the bushes.

Hop-along turned to the Ewe-ni-horn, and, even though his throat was bleeding and he couldn't talk, he found himself formulating thoughts of thanks. They were thoughts that the sheep seemed to be able to understand, but it didn't respond. Instead, it lowered its head and took off at great speed towards the farm.

It was only then that Hop-along heard the sound of barking. Looking back down the valley, he saw a pack of dogs running towards him, closely followed by a group of horsemen. Taking off after the Ewe-ni-horn, he jumped a small stream and followed it into a field in which there was a large flock of sheep.

The sheep scattered, but didn't panic, as Hop-along hobbled among them. Nor did they seem to notice that another sheep had joined them, even though it had a horn where it should have had a tail.

Before they closed in again as one flock, Hop-along paused and looked back. The horsemen had pulled up at the stream, while their dogs were milling around, barking, having been told to heel. It was obvious that the riders wanted to follow the Ewe-ni-horn into the field, but were of two minds about what to do. A bit like the Dillylama, Hop-along thought. He smiled and hobbled on. He knew, just as well as the horsemen knew, that if they followed him in among the flock they would be risking the ire of the farmer. In any event, how would they ever find a Ewe-ni-horn in a flock of sheep?

9

The Liesalot Liesalot

There was a rainbow in the meadow, even though the sun was shining from a clear blue sky and there wasn't a hint of rain. It wasn't a big rainbow, but it had all the colours of what the foxes call 'the bow in the sky'. It arched above the clump of superweeds at the bend in the river, and it was caused by droplets of liquid that were man-made. The man from the big house had found, to his alarm, that his experiments had created superweeds, and now, in a desperate effort to kill them, he had created a superweed-killer. As he sprayed it up into the summer air, in an effort to reach the topmost leaves and blossoms, the fine mist caught the rays of the sun and dispersed them into a glistening array of colour.

Unlike nature's rainbow, which arches across the earth itself and lingers long enough to tantalise those who live below, the small bow in the meadow quickly dissolved with the spray. As it did so, the man looked across the river and scanned the far side of the valley. There was no sign of his other creations, those that had escaped from his enclosure, and, with a furtive look around to make sure he wasn't being observed, he made his way back across the fields to the big house.

When the man had gone, another of his creations — one he had forgotten about — slipped quietly out of the clump of superweeds and loped into the long grass. Had the man braved the stench of the rubbish he had dumped there and bothered to look inside the clump of weeds, he would have found that the Fo-paw had formed a strange alliance with the rabbit-eating sundew. However, he was in a hurry to get back to his laboratory. Later he would return to make sure his superweed-killer had done its work.

It was coming on towards evening, and a gentle breeze was still caressing the leaves as the two fox cubs trotted through the trees. Between them was another creature, who was different in almost every way from the foxes. Whereas each of the cubs had a long flowing tail, he had a short straight one — one that should have been curly but wasn't — and while they had fine, pointed noses, he had two noses in one, noses so blunt they were known as snouts.

The cubs had taken an instant liking to the pig, not only because he too was young, but because he seemed to have the answers to many of the questions they wanted to ask. It also intrigued them greatly that he had two faces and was able to look at, and talk to, both of them at the same time. That was why they were now trotting along with the pig in the middle.

Having heard from their elders that the pig was a very intelligent animal, the cubs took the opportunity to try and find the answer to a question that had been puzzling them for some time. The same question had also been puzzling the older foxes, ever since it had been posed by Old Sage Brush.

'Gaze-pig?' said Blaze. When the pig grunted as if to ask what she wanted, she continued, 'Remember the egg we were telling you about — the one we found at the bend in the river? Was it laid by the Liesalot?'

'I don't think so,' the pig replied. 'At least, I've never seen it lay an egg. But I know it has a memory of such an egg.'

'How do you know?' asked Firefly.

'Because I have heard it speak of it,' said the pig. 'At least, I have heard one of its heads speak of such an egg.'

'And what does the other head say?' asked Blaze.

'The other head says it has no such recollection,' the pig grunted. 'But then, it always says the opposite of what the first one says, so I wouldn't pay much attention to that.'

The pig stopped for a moment to root under a bush for something his super-sensitive sense of smell had told him was there. As he gulped it down, Blaze asked, 'If an egg is broken, how can you put it together again?'

The pig snorted and laughed. 'Why should you want to put an egg together again?'

'It's Old Sage Brush,' Firefly explained. 'He told the older foxes that man can break an egg, but he cannot put it together again.'

'He said only one creature can do that,' said Blaze. 'But which one? None of us — not even the older foxes — can figure it out.'

The pig laughed with both of his faces until his hairy shoulders shook, and trotted on.

'Well?' asked Blaze, as she hurried to catch up. 'Which one is it?'

The pig smiled at both of them and said, 'Sure, that's obvious.'

The cubs stopped and looked at each other in a way that said it wasn't a bit obvious — at least, not to them. But when they caught up with him again, he refused to tell them. He said they should do as the old fox had told them and figure it out for themselves.

They trotted on, and Firefly said, 'Gaze-pig?' When the pig grunted again, she continued, 'Is it true that you see yourself running like the wind and sailing over the fences like a gazehound?'

'What's a gazehound?' asked the pig.

'It's a long, thin hound that hunts hares,' Firefly explained.

'We've never seen one ourselves,' said Blaze. 'But Father has. He told us all about it.'

'He said it hunts with its eyes instead of its nose,' continued Firefly. 'It has very sharp teeth, and it's very fast — faster than a fox.'

'It can even catch a hare,' said Blaze, 'and you know how fast they are.'

The pig grunted. Having been reared at the big house and spent his life in an enclosure, he had never seen a hare, not to mention a gazehound. However, he did have a memory of another existence — a memory of a time when he could run fast and jump so high he could clear a five-barred gate. He could not know that this memory had been passed down to him in the genes of a sow whose ancestor had been so agile that man had called it a greyhound pig.

'It's true,' he told the cubs, 'I sometimes see myself running across the fields, but I don't know if it's like this gazehound you tell me about. I'm running like the wind and jumping all the gates and fences I come to. But it's just a dream.'

'Hop-along had a dream like that,' said Blaze. 'Only it wasn't a dream. At least, not all of it.'

The pig chuckled. 'Well, even with two faces I can't see myself doing what I do in my dreams.'

The cubs couldn't imagine it either, so they laughed and trotted on beside their strange friend until they arrived at the oak tree where Old Sage Brush lived. Black Tip and Vickey, having no earth of their own now, were staying with the old fox. Sinnéad and Skulking Dog were also there, and they were all deep in conversation.

'We were just saying, Gaze-pig,' Old Sage Brush told him, 'that we made a big mistake in forgetting about this other creature — what was it Hop-along said it was called?'

'The Fo-paw?' said the pig.

'That's it,' said the old fox. 'The Fo-paw. Hop-along says it nearly killed him.'

'I forgot about it too,' admitted the Gaze-pig. 'It's just that it's not really one of us. It's a loner. It does its own thing.'

'And that,' said Old Sage Brush, 'makes it all the more dangerous.'

'So what can we do to keep it away from us?' asked Black Tip.

The old fox stroked his grey whiskers with his paw before replying, 'We must always keep our friends close to us, but our enemies even closer.'

'What do you mean?' asked Sinnéad.

'What I mean,' explained Old Sage Brush, 'is that we can keep this Fo-paw away from us by keeping a close eye on it. But first we must find it.' He turned to the pig. 'Now, Gaze-pig, have you any idea where its lair might be?'

'I'm sorry,' replied the pig. 'While the Liesalot and the Dillylama have two heads and I have two faces, they are the heads and faces of our own breeds. The Fo-paw has one head, but it is the head of two hunters, and it has a mind of its own.'

'Well,' said Skulking Dog, 'it's my guess that its den is somewhere on the far side of the river. The rabbits are still running scared over there, so that's where it must be doing most of its hunting.'

'Wherever it is,' the old fox told them, 'we must find it. This time it's our strongest, not our weakest, that we must send.'

Knowing that he was referring to Black Tip and Skulking Dog, Vickey and Sinnéad volunteered to go with them.

Old Sage Brush agreed, saying, 'All right, but the Fo-paw seems to have enough cunning and strength for two, so be careful.' The cubs immediately jumped up, asking if they could go too, but the old fox forbade it and they quickly lay down again.

'Well, Gaze-pig,' said Old Sage Brush, when the others had gone, 'what news do you bring?'

The cubs listened as the pig told the old fox that, while the Liesalot and the Dillylama had agreed to stay in the quarry until dark, he couldn't be sure that they would do so. 'It's difficult to know with the Liesalot,' he explained. 'One head says one thing and the other head says another. As for the Dillylama, it'll probably do whatever the Liesalot does. It's almost incapable of making up its own mind.'

Old Sage Brush nodded. 'All right, I'll go down and see them myself.' This was a phrase that the old fox often used, and it always intrigued the cubs, as they knew he couldn't see, but they said nothing. 'Maybe,' he added, 'I can talk sense into one of their heads.'

Old Sage Brush and the pig talked for a while longer. Then the old fox sniffed the air a few times and decided it was time to go. The cubs, he said, should note that the warm summer air had cooled and the breeze had died down. That meant there would be less scent, and less danger that it would be carried to their enemies — an important consideration for a young fox or a frail old fox like himself.

Hop-along was still licking his wounds in his earth up at the blackthorns when the cubs called to say that Old Sage Brush wanted him to join them in the quarry. Because of his frustrating experience with the Ewe-ni-horn and his bruising encounter with the Fo-paw, Hop-along was now even less enamoured of the creatures from the big house. He was also feeling somewhat sorry for himself, and when he arrived at the quarry, he took care to sit well back from the four heads of the two creatures that were still there.

The cubs had not been told that they could come to the quarry too, but they came anyway. Being young and inexperienced, they were less cautious than Hop-along, and when they lay down beside the Dillylama, they found it had a strange way of repelling those who came too near it. Without warning, one of its heads snorted and sneezed, and the cubs found themselves being sprayed with an unpleasant mixture of chewed-up grass and saliva. At the same time, the Liesalot stretched out both its long necks and began pecking them. The pig, who had settled down at a safe distance with Old Sage Brush, grunted, and as the cubs beat a hasty retreat they could see there was a gleam of amusement in at least two of his three eyes. Feeling somewhat chastened, they lay down behind the pig and the old fox and wondered what was going to happen next.

For a moment, nothing was said, and as the cubs waited, they watched the two heads of the Dillylama with great curiosity. Its big lips and nostrils were raised as it continued to chew, and it stared at the foxes with eyes that were as big and brown as chestnuts. At the same time, the Liesalot nibbled continuously with both its beaks at any grass or leaves that came within its reach.

'Did you tell them about the fun dogs?' Old Sage Brush asked the pig.

The Gaze-pig nodded his two faces and was about to reply when Hop-along cleared his aching throat and, speaking hoarsely, whispered, 'They weren't really fun dogs. Not the type man uses when he's digging us out for fun. They were more ... well, sort of funny dogs.'

'Still, they chased you and the Ewe-ni-horn,' the old fox reminded him. 'And, Liesalot,' he said, turning to the big bird, 'they'll chase you and your friend too, if you don't stay here until dark.'

The Liesalot lifted its two heads to listen, and the cubs could see it swallowing a ball of grass and leaves down each of its two throats. They could also see that its four round eyes had lashes and that they seemed to blink as they stared. In response to what the old fox had said, it curled its long necks around each other, one of its heads saying, 'I have been chased before — across the sands and the tall grass. But I can run faster than the striped horse, and man has never caught me.'

As this head continued to recall a previous existence in which it saw itself in the Land of the Zebra, the other head recalled a memory of a circus, saying, 'I too have been chased by man, but he has caught me. I see him astride my back, riding me around and around in circles the way he rides a horse.'

The two heads turned inwards to look at each other.

'If man cannot catch me,' said the first, 'I see no need to hide.'

'I do,' said the second, 'so I am staying here.'

The bird then uncoiled its two long necks, and those who watched couldn't tell which head had said what.

Old Sage Brush shifted uncomfortably, frustrated by what he was hearing and annoyed with himself that he could not see. 'Well, which is it?' he asked. 'Are you going to stay hidden or not?'

When there was no answer from the bird, the pig said, 'There's no telling what it's going to do! You can believe one head, but not the other. But whether either one intends to stay, even I, with my two faces and three eyes, cannot tell.'

'And how about the Dillylama?' asked the old fox. 'Will it agree to stay out of sight?'

The Dillylama began to say something, but it was only a nervous stutter.

'It'll probably do what the Liesalot does,' the pig told him.

'Well, Gaze-pig, try and get them to stay here until it's dark,' said Old Sage Brush firmly. 'Otherwise they'll bring man and his fun dogs down on all of us.'

The pig lifted his three eyes up to the sky in a gesture that showed his own frustration and, as the old fox turned to go, said, 'I'll try, but I can't promise they'll do it.'

Five pairs of soft brown eyes, as big and round as ripe hazelnuts, watched the world outside from the safety of the entrance to their burrow. While the summer sun had beckoned the young rabbits to come out and bask in its life-giving warmth, they had stayed in their home under the Hill of Hazels throughout the day. Only now, when the warmth of the sun had been sapped by the growth of the day and its light began to fade, were the young rabbits allowed to venture above ground. Their elders had warned them about a strange creature that had come to the valley, a stealthy hunter that would devour them if they didn't stay below ground and do as they were told.

As the foxes watched, other eyes appeared at the many entrances to the warren in the side of the hill. They were older, more experienced eyes, and, above them, ears that were long and thin and almost transparent swivelled to the sounds of the approaching dusk, each ear turning independently as it scanned its surroundings to help the eyes detect any possible sources of danger. At the same time, the whiskered noses of the rabbits twitched as if they were constantly sniffing the evening breeze, but it was their ears and eyes that would tell them when to take their first timid hops out into the field to nibble the grass.

Unaware that the foxes were watching them, one of the older rabbits hopped down the flattened clay that formed the pathway to its burrow. It paused, its long ears still held high and turning to every sound. Hearing nothing that suggested any danger, it hopped forward again, followed by another rabbit, and another. Soon, many members of the warren were nibbling at the grass, or standing on their hind legs to pick at the new shoots and leaves on tiny saplings growing at the edge of the hazels. Others, the foxes could see, were sniffing through their droppings, ignoring those that were firm and dry and eating the ones that were soft and black. It was a ritual in which the rabbits passed their droppings through their digestive systems a second time, so as to reclaim any protein that had escaped the first time and use valuable food that would otherwise be wasted. However, it was a trait that was not common to the foxes and one which caused them great amusement.

The rabbits would have been intrigued had they known that the foxes were watching, yet not attacking them. And they would have been even more reluctant to come out had they known that the foxes were waiting for the other hunter to come — the one that had made them afraid to venture out during the day and had become the subject of stories that made their young shiver in their nests. Few had seen the creature, and those who had had described a hunter the like of which none of them had ever seen before.

Nor had the foxes seen what they had come to call 'the Fo-paw', and as they waited for it to come, they tried to imagine what it looked like. From what Hop-along had said, they knew it had the nose of a fox but the short ears of a cat, the long-haired fur of a fox but the sloping tail of a cat. Still, they found it difficult to imagine, and they waited with bated breath in the hope that it would come for the rabbits. Then they could follow it and find out where it had made its den.

The Fo-paw, however, had devised a plan by which the rabbits would come to it!

In their search for the Fo-paw's den, the foxes had ranged far and wide, but they had failed to look in the one place where it felt it would be safe. Because of the stench, they had stayed clear of the clump of super-weeds down in the meadow. But, because of the stench, the Fo-paw knew its scent would not be detected there.

Furthermore, it had noticed that, with the approach of dusk, some of the rabbits from the warren on the hill would come there and try to drink from the sundew flowers.

Now, as one rabbit, then another, hopped into the clump of weeds, the Fo-paw watched and waited. Only the merest flick of the end of its sweeping tail betrayed its intention, but the rabbits didn't see it. They had eyes only for the glistening beads on the sundew. Slowly but surely, the flower lured them to it with the promise of droplets of water.

When, with a final hop, the first rabbit found to its cost that they were not droplets of water but a sticky substance that held it fast, its friends on the Hill of Hazels heard it scream and bolted back into their burrows. Even as they did so, they heard a second scream. Like a cat pouncing on a mouse, the Fo-paw had sprung upon the other rabbit as it tried to escape.

Up at the warren, the foxes thought they were hearing the death-cry of only one rabbit. Having seen the work of the sundew plant before, they sat tight and waited. They didn't realise that, when silence returned to the meadow, the Fo-paw, like the sundew, was enjoying its first full meal of the day, while they went hungry.

By this time, the sun had almost disappeared behind the hills. Looking across the valley towards the black-thorns, the foxes saw, to their dismay, that the Liesalot and the Dillylama had come down to the meadows to graze. They immediately abandoned their search for the Fo-paw and hurried back across the river.

It was, they told the Liesalot, too early to come out, as there was still light enough for man to see them. However, both heads on both creatures ignored them and continued to graze as if they hadn't eaten for days.

Suddenly, the Liesalot raised its long necks and exclaimed, 'Man is coming! Man is coming!'

'Which way?' asked Skulking Dog.

The Liesalot twisted its long necks around each other, and one of the heads looked towards the Hill of Hazels, saying, 'That way,' but the other head pointed its beak in the opposite direction and told him, 'That way.' It then unravelled its necks, and the foxes were unable to tell which head had said what. Rooted to the ground, they could only stand and watch, mesmerised, as the Liesalot flapped its short wings and proceeded to run back and forth across the meadow like a headless chicken. At the same time, the Dillylama, true to form, pranced around and around in a circle as if it couldn't make up its mind which way to run.

The foxes didn't know which way to run either. They looked around but could see no sign of man, nor could they scent any sign of danger. Frustrated and alarmed, they bolted away through the long meadow grass and headed up towards the blackthorns.

From the Hill of Hazels, the man from the big house watched the Liesalot and the Dillylama. He was relieved that, at long last, he had spotted them, but he wondered what the Liesalot was doing, running back and forth as if it was in a panic. He didn't know that the big bird, like the ostrich from which it had been cloned, could focus on objects up to two miles away with telescopic precision, and had become aware of his presence on the hill. Nor did he know that it was struggling to cope with two instincts. One instinct was telling it to run towards him, as it had so often at the big house, when he had come to feed it. The other was telling it to run to the freedom it seemed to recall, in a sun-bleached plain, somewhere in a previous existence.

The man's senses were not as keen as those of the Liesalot, and, at that distance and in the fading light, he didn't see the foxes. All he saw was his two creations eventually making up their minds and running up towards the blackthorns. Now, he thought, his friends from the circus would know where to find them. While they were doing that, he would have to take further steps to destroy the clump of superweeds in the meadow. They had resisted his superweed-killer, and he realised that the only way to get rid of them was to burn them.

On reaching the old quarry up at the blackthorns, Black Tip and his friends looked back and found that the Liesalot and the Dillylama were following them. There was no sign of man, but they realised that, if he had seen the two creatures in the meadow, it would only be a matter of time before he came to the black-thorns looking for them. Somehow, they told one another, they would have to find out how to tell which head of the Liesalot told the truth and which head didn't; otherwise it could put them all in danger. And trying to sort out the heads of the Liesalot, they knew, would be as difficult as trying to figure out how to put an egg back together again!

10

A Tale of Two Heads

A pied wagtail walked jerkily across the clearing. Flicking its tail up and down, it stopped now and then to pick up a morsel of food so tiny only it could see it. The wagtail could hear the foxes talking in the earth beneath the gnarled roots of the oak tree, but it ignored them and hopped up onto the edge of an eggshell so large it couldn't see it. At least, it couldn't see the shell for what it was, but it knew there was rainwater in it, and, despite the presence of the foxes, it took its first sip of the day, then fluttered off about its business.

Hop-along, who was lying in the long grass at the end of the clearing, watched the wagtail go, and when it had disappeared through the trees, he looked up to see the long-tailed tits flitting among the higher branches. Their tails had become straight again, and he wondered if that was because their young had fledged and they were no longer nesting. He also wondered why some birds had long tails and some had short tails. The magpie had a long tail and the crow had a short tail, and yet he had seen the crow fly longer journeys than the magpie. And why did some birds flick their tails so much? Some birds with long tails, like the magpie, were always flicking them, but the cock pheasant had an even longer tail, which it didn't flick. The long-tailed tit didn't flick its tail either — at least, not the way the wagtail did, and the wagtail had a much shorter tail.

Whatever the answer was, Hop-along knew tails were important. The tail of the fox was very important, especially when it came to chasing a rabbit or running from the gazehounds. He recalled once knowing a fox without a tail. What was his name?

Hop-along got up and was about to go over to the oak tree to ask his friends, when he thought better of it. They were deep in conversation with Old Sage Brush, and he didn't want to interrupt them, so he lay down again and thought about it a little longer.

What was his name? he thought. Stumpy — that was it. What else? He was a fine little fox. Had his tail cut off when he was chased by man and the howling dogs. It hadn't helped his balance much, especially when he had to make a tight turn at high speed. But he had survived.

Resting his nose on his own tail, Hop-along realised that, while he had been looking at birds and thinking of foxes, it was another creature that was on his mind — one with the body of a fox but the long, sloping tail of a cat. He had heard his friends tell Old Sage

Brush how it had the rabbits over at the Hill of Hazels frightened to death, and how they had failed to find it. Yet it had found him. It had sought him out as the weakest of the foxes, and it had come after him.

Hop-along sighed. If it hadn't been for him, his friends would never have known that the creatures at the big house even existed. The creatures wouldn't have come to the blackthorns, and the foxes wouldn't be in this predicament. He had put them all in danger, especially Old Sage Brush. If man and his dogs didn't come across the old fox, the Fo-paw would seek him out. That was the sort of creature it was. First it would come for the one with three legs, then for the one that was old, then .... Hop-along paused. Blaze and Firefly would be vulnerable too ... and their mother. Flame, he knew, was still not fully recovered from the ordeal of rearing the cubs, and wasn't yet strong enough to hunt for herself — or to defend herself.

Getting up, Hop-along hobbled over to the eggshell for a drink of rainwater. As he turned to go, Black Tip emerged from the earth and asked him to give a message to the Gaze-pig on his way back to the blackthorns. He promised he would. But after delivering the message, he turned his back to the blackthorns, made his way down to the meadows and crossed the river.

~

The other foxes had been telling Old Sage Brush about their efforts to locate the Fo-paw. They had, they explained, refrained from catching any of the rabbits themselves, in the hope that the Fo-paw might do so.

'But it didn't turn up,' added Sinnéad. 'So we don't

even have a rabbit for you. Sorry.'

The old fox turned to his daughter, and even though he couldn't see her, he smiled. 'No need to apologise. It was a good idea, and it just might have worked.'

'We got a dreadful shock when we saw those creatures down in the meadows,' Vickey told him.

'And when the Liesalot told us man was coming,' said Black Tip, 'we didn't know which way to run.'

'One head told us he was coming from one direction,' Skulking Dog recalled, 'and the other head told us the complete opposite.'

Vickey sighed a sigh of exasperation. 'We'll have to try and figure out which head is telling the truth and which head isn't.'

'Otherwise we'll run straight into trouble,' said Black Tip.

Knowing that there was no fox wiser than her father, Sinnéad shuffled closer to him and asked, 'Is there no way we can tell?'

'The problem is,' said Skulking Dog, before the old fox could answer, 'it has this awful habit of twisting its necks around each other.'

'And then, when it undoes them,' said Black Tip, 'we can't tell which head has said what.'

'Surely there must be some way of telling one from the other,' added Vickey.

'Just as there is a time for everything,' Old Sage Brush told them, 'there is an answer for everything.' He raised his grey head as if his unseeing eyes were looking for inspiration from the great god Vulpes. 'The problem is, some things take longer to figure out than others. And time is something we haven't got. Unless that bird has the sense to stay where it is.'

Vickey snorted. 'The only one who has any sense is the pig.'

'And he has had more time than any of us to observe the Liesalot,' said Old Sage Brush. 'Maybe he has figured out how to tell which head is telling the truth.'

When the pig got Hop-along's message, he urged the Liesalot and the Dillylama to remain in the quarry until he returned, and hurried up through the wood to the old oak tree. There he lay down and waited until the foxes came out of the earth. With one eye he watched Black Tip and Vickey settle to one side of him, with another he watched Skulking Dog and Sinnéad settle to the other side of him, and with the eye in the middle of his two faces, he watched Old Sage Brush settle down in front of him.

'Well, Gaze-pig?' said the old fox, when they had explained their dilemma to him. 'I know there is a way to overcome this problem with the Liesalot. But it is a matter that requires much thought. And unless that bird has a grain of wisdom in one of its heads — which I doubt — then it will put us in even more danger than we are in now.'

The pig nodded. 'Yes, the Liesalot can be a very annoying bird, all right. I should know. I have lived close to it for a long time. But I have also observed it closely with both of my faces, and I have thought about it deeply with both of my minds — and, yes, there is a way.'

'You mean,' asked Vickey, 'there's a way to tell which head is telling the truth and which is telling a lie?'

The pig shook both its heads. 'No. I didn't say that. What I said was, there is a way.'

'There is a way to what?' asked Sinnéad.

'Be patient,' said Old Sage Brush. 'Let the Gaze-pig say what he has to say.'

The pig smiled with both of his faces, even though he knew the old fox couldn't see him, and continued,

'There is no way to tell which head is telling the truth and which is telling a lie. But there is a way to determine the truth of what they say.'

The foxes waited, and when the pig said no more, Black Tip asked, 'So what is it?'

'Well,' the pig replied, 'it's best to wait until it has uncurled its necks. Then there is a question you can ask that will give you the answer.'

'And which head do you ask?' Skulking Dog wanted to know.

'It doesn't matter,' said the pig.

'But how can you put a question to either head that will give you the right answer?' asked Sinnéad.

'Let the Gaze-pig answer,' Old Sage Brush told them. 'Then you will know what question to ask.'

The pig smiled again with both his faces, saying, 'It's very simple, really.'

The foxes looked at one another and wondered if they would ever hear what it was the pig was going to tell them.

'It really is,' the pig assured them, seeing with the eyes on the sides of his faces that they were becoming impatient. 'You simply ask one of the Liesalot's heads what the other one would say.'

'Is that it?' asked Skulking Dog.

The question was addressed to the pig, but Old Sage Brush answered, 'Ah yes, that's it.'

'You see,' said the pig, seeing that they didn't see, 'if the Liesalot says it sees man coming and you want to know which way, you ask one of the heads which way the other head says he's coming. If you're asking the head that tells the truth, it will ask the one that is telling lies, and so it will reply truthfully, but the answer will be a lie. And if you are asking the head that tells lies, it will ask the one that tells the truth, but reply untruthfully, and the answer will also be a lie. So, whatever answer you get, you know the opposite is the truth. As I said before, it's simple.'

The foxes looked at one another in a way that clearly said that what the pig had told them was anything but simple, but they said nothing, for they were going over in their minds what he had been trying to tell them. 'If you're speaking to the one that tells the truth, it will tell you a lie ... and if you're speaking to the one that tells lies, it will tell you a lie, so ....'

'That's it, then,' said the old fox, 'so stop your mumbling. You simply ask one head what the other head would say, and, whatever answer you get, you know it's a lie. Well done, Gaze-pig. You may not have the cunning or the speed of a fox, but you have a mind — or should I say minds — that any fox would envy.'

The pig smiled, and as he got up to return to the quarry, he said, 'Sometimes I imagine I have the speed, too, but then, that must be all in my mind — or should I say my minds!'

Old Sage Brush laughed, and the others, who were still trying to tease out in their own minds how the question they would put to the Liesalot would work, followed him back down into the earth beneath the oak tree.

The Land of Sinna, it seemed, was covered with dandelion clocks, and as Black Tip and Vickey looked down the side of the valley, clouds of seeds drifted across the fields. The dandelion clocks, they could see, were being disturbed by four of the biggest toes that had ever set foot in the valley, and by eight so fine and timid they would have suited a sheep.

Whatever about the Dillylama, the foxes realised that the Liesalot did not have in either of its heads the grain of sense that Old Sage Brush wished it had. Whichever god had created this creature, they could see he had deprived it of wisdom. Nor had he imparted to it the understanding that other creatures might have expected. And while he had bestowed a fine tail on the rainbow bird, he had left this one with little or none. Nor had he given it the wings to fly. Instead, he had endowed it with two long legs and two large feet with which to tread the land. And, as if that wasn't bad enough, he had given it two long necks and two small heads, both of which it lifted high to scorn all who lived below.

Soon, the two foxes would learn, the Liesalot would even scorn the strength of the horse and frighten it just as easily as it was frightening the grasshopper that was now hopping farther than it had ever hopped before, in an effort to avoid the two large toes which this strange bird had on each of its feet.

She-la, who had been out hunting, had returned to the blackthorns with a rabbit for Hop-along and the cubs, only to be told by the cubs that her mate had gone up to visit Old Sage Brush. Seeing that the Liesalot and the Dillylama had gone out to the fields to graze, and realising the danger this might bring upon them, she gave the rabbit to the cubs, warned them not to leave the earth, and followed Hop-along's scent up to the wood. There she met Skulking Dog and Sinnéad, who told her that her mate had been up at the oak tree but had left to give a message to the Gaze-pig. Where he was now, they didn't know. They had assumed that he was returning to the blackthorns. Maybe, they told her, he had gone hunting.

As She-la raced away to try and locate her mate, Skulking Dog and Sinnéad looked at the two creatures that were grazing on the side of the valley for all to see. The Dillylama, they knew, wasn't to blame. It just did whatever the Liesalot did, and they wondered, just as Black Tip and Vickey had wondered, how such a tall bird could have such shortcomings. The more they thought about it, the more it seemed to them that nature, for once, was not on their side. While they had urged the Liesalot and the Dillylama to stay in the quarry during the day and come out to graze at night, nature had told them otherwise. It had told them there was a time to eat and a time to sleep, and nothing else seemed to matter — not even the danger that man might come after them in the same way that he had come after the Ewe-ni-horn.

The foxes had no way of knowing how long the Liesalot and the Dillylama had been grazing in the open, but they thought that if they had eaten enough, perhaps they could be persuaded to return to the quarry before it was too late. What none of them realised was that, when it came to eating, neither the Liesalot nor the Dillylama ever had enough.

Having gorged themselves on the rabbit, Blaze and Firefly crept out of the blackthorns, curious to know why She-la had taken off so quickly. To their surprise, they saw that the Liesalot and the Dillylama had left the quarry and were grazing a few fields farther down. With even greater curiosity, they watched as Black Tip and Vickey approached the two creatures from one direction and Skulking Dog and Sinnéad approached from another.

Because it was facing two ways at the same time, it was the Dillylama that first noticed the foxes, and even though they were a familiar sight at this stage, it was still suspicious of them. Unlike the Liesalot or the Gaze-pig or the Ewe-ni-horn, it had never spoken to them, beyond giving a soft sort of moan, and now it pranced around in a circle as if it was preparing to run, spitting half-chewed grass as it did so. The Liesalot, on the other hand, continued to nibble at the grass with both its heads, raising its long necks now and again to swallow what it had collected in each of its beaks. Only when the foxes came too close did it reach out and peck at them. Then it would stop grazing for a moment, raise its heads and stare at them with its dark, round eyes, all of which seemed to have a continuous blinking movement, even though they stayed wide open.

Vickey was about to tell the Liesalot that it would be safer if they returned to the quarry, when the bird, whose heads were still raised high, wrapped its necks around each other and exclaimed, 'Man is coming! Man is coming!' The two heads, she saw, were facing in opposite directions, one looking over a nearby hedge, the other towards the wood.

On hearing this, the Dillylama became even more agitated, and the foxes could see it was about to take off. It too was tall enough to see which way man was coming, but even so, it was waiting to find out from the Liesalot which way it should run.

The foxes were also waiting to see which way they should run, and it seemed an age before the big bird uncoiled its necks. Vickey immediately asked the nearest head, 'Which way does your other head say man is coming?'

For a split second the two heads looked at each other, and, whatever type of communication occurred, the head to which the question had been directed replied, 'That way,' and pointed towards the wood. For a moment, the foxes stood rooted to the spot, going over in their minds what the pig had told them. If the head they were talking to was the one that told the truth, then it was relating truthfully what the other had said, and that was a lie. And if it was the head that told lies, then it was not relating truthfully what the other had said. In either event, as the pig had said, what they were being told was a lie. Man was not coming from the wood, but from the opposite direction.

The four foxes turned as one and raced up through the fields towards the wood. A short time later, they turned and looked back. To their relief, they found that they had run in the right direction, but to their surprise they saw that the Liesalot had chosen the open fields. Steering itself with its short wings, it had taken off at great speed along the side of the valley. As for the Dillylama, it was running back and forth across the field where it had been grazing, unable to make up its mind which way to go. Fortunately for it, man had seen the Liesalot first and was giving chase, his horses at full stretch, his dogs in full cry.

Never before had the Land of Sinna seen such a hunt. Man had, on occasion, come to the valley to hunt the hares, and he had, on many occasions, come to hunt the fox. But never before had he come to hunt a bird which had legs as long as those of his horse — and which, as he was about to discover, could run faster! Nothing seemed to stop the Liesalot, or even slow its stride, and soon the riders and their dogs found themselves falling farther and farther behind. Swerving this way and that, the big bird kept up a dizzy speed and disappeared over the brow of a hill. When, a short time later, the riders arrived at the spot, it was nowhere to be seen.

While the Liesalot might have lacked the wisdom and the cunning of the fox, it was, in its own peculiar way, doing what its ancestors would have done on the dusty plains of Africa. It was simply using its speed to outrun its enemies, and on reaching the hill, it had looked out on what its instinct told it was a way of escape. And so, while another animal of its size would have kept well away from the bog that stretched out before it, the Liesalot, thinking it was a place where it could muster even more speed, had raced down towards it. But — unlike the moorhen, whose toes are spread out to allow it to walk on the flimsiest of surfaces — an ostrich has only two toes, which are close together and point forward to allow it to run on a hard surface.

The Liesalot had gone only a few strides into the bog when its narrow feet cut through the surface and it began to sink. Soon it found it couldn't move. Its wings were too short to give it any leverage, and so it did what its memory of a previous existence told it to do. It lay down as flat as it could and stretched its long necks out in front of it. The big bird had no way of knowing that it was this behaviour that had given the ostrich the reputation of hiding its head in the sand. It just knew that this was what it had to do, and if either of its heads had had the capacity to hope, it would have hoped that man wouldn't see it.

Man, indeed, would not have seen the Liesalot, for as he looked out across the bog one hump of heather looked much the same as another. However, his dogs were slightly more perceptive, and, even though they were not hunting-dogs, it wasn't long before they came across the Liesalot lying not far from the edge. One of the riders immediately produced a lasso, the two necks were tied together as one, and, after a lot of pulling and shoving, the Liesalot was dragged clear. It immediately began kicking and pecking at the horses and ponies, which shied away, unseating several of their riders.

During a lifetime in the circus, however, one of the riders had dealt with such a bird before. As it missed its footing and almost sank to the ground, he took hold of the lasso and pulled himself up onto its back. The Liesalot immediately took off across the fields, and a short time later, the two cubs, who were watching from the entrance to their earth, were astonished to see it racing up towards the blackthorns, man riding it as he would a horse. Thinking that it was heading for the safety of the old quarry, they waited with bated breath.

But the Liesalot wasn't stopping, not even for the blackthorns. As the cubs dived for cover, it crashed through the thorn-bushes, brushing off the rider and escaping through the far side.

It seemed a long time before the other riders arrived to lift their friend out of the blackthorns, and by then even the Dillylama had made up its mind where it should hide. Because of the thorns that were now in his body, the unfortunate rider could no longer ride, and as he was helped away by his friends, there was a grunt and a chuckle from further up the blackthorns. The Gaze-pig hadn't seen everything that had happened. But he had seen some of it, and he couldn't help thinking that maybe the man — if he had known how — should have asked the Liesalot's permission before climbing onto its back. But then, even if one of its heads had given him permission, how would he have known if it was telling the truth?

11

The Dance of the Dillylama

A magpie landed precariously on what it took to be a rowan tree, only to find that what it had mistaken for rowan berries were the floral seeds of a tall yellow weed. Had the magpie given the matter any thought, it would have wondered why this weed had grown so high and flowered so early. It might even have recognised the weed as one that abounds in midsummer, a flower of the fields that grows undisturbed by grazing animals. It might also have recognised the large striped caterpillar that was crawling up the stem. But, whether the caterpillar was too big, or whether its black and yellow stripes showed that it was poisonous, the magpie left it alone. With a flick of its long blue-black tail, it hopped over onto the giant thistle that grew nearby, leaving the caterpillar of the Cinnabar moth to the equally poisonous plant that man calls ragwort.

With its usual curiosity, the magpie examined the purple flower-heads of the thistle. Making sure it avoided the sharp, spear-like leaves, it pecked at the spiny flowers and wondered if they would soon release their seeds. Not that it could eat such huge seeds. It was, as always, just curious. For a moment it balanced precariously in the breeze. Then, with a harsh squawk, it took to the air, spread its tail and fluttered uncertainly away towards the trees at the big house.

All this, Hop-along observed from the Hill of Hazels. Having settled himself in the long grass at the top, he closed his eyes and listened to the wind. Now that he had decided what he must do, he knew that the wind was his only friend. As he cocked his ear to the summer breeze and caressed it with his nose, he thought of that other time he had crossed the river. For whatever reason, he had found himself being carried across the hills and meadows, touching the ground only now and again, and with four fine paws. It was the wind, he recalled, that had picked him up and made him one with Mother Earth, and he knew he must rely on it again if he was to survive what had to be done.

Perhaps, Hop-along thought, he should have told She-la what he was going to do — or even consulted Old Sage Brush. But then, he told himself, they would have talked him out of it. He was also convinced that his friends were wasting their time looking for the Fo-paw. They would never find it. But one thing he knew for certain — the Fo-paw would look for him.

Having heard how to determine the truth of what the Liesalot was saying, the cubs were asking it all sorts of questions to see if they could come up with the right answers. The man who had dared to use the Liesalot as a horse had failed to notice the fox earth beneath the blackthorns, so concerned had he been with his own problems, but it was a long time before the cubs had ventured out. When they did so, they saw the Liesalot, its heads hung low so as not to be seen, returning to the quarry, and when the Gaze-pig followed it, so did they.

The Dillylama, having made up its own mind for once, was already back in the quarry, and it moaned softly and stared with its large brown eyes as the cubs asked the Liesalot where man and his dogs had gone. When the Liesalot twisted its necks around each other and gave contradictory answers, the cubs realised they had not posed the right question.

Glancing at the Gaze-pig to see if they were doing the right thing, they waited until the bird had uncurled its necks and they were able to address the nearest head.

'Which way does your other head say man has gone?' Blaze asked it.

The nearest head consulted the other head and looked up towards the hill, saying, 'That way.'

The cubs smiled. They knew, from the formula the pig had given, that the riders had gone in the other direction, probably across the river to the big house.

And so the game went on, until the Liesalot wrapped its two necks around each other and refused to answer any more questions. At the same time, the Dillylama spat at the cubs to show its displeasure at what they were doing, and the Gaze-pig told them, 'Better leave the bird alone. Can't you see it's tired?'

A short time later, She-la arrived, and, having asked

the Gaze-pig if he had seen Hop-along, she took the cubs and returned to the blackthorns. Vickey and Sinnéad arrived a short time later and informed the pig that Black Tip and Skulking Dog had agreed to go and look for Hop-along. They just hoped they would find him before the Fo-paw did.

As they settled down in the undergrowth on the side of the quarry, the vixens noticed what the cubs, in their immaturity, had failed to notice. The Liesalot, they thought, looked very tired — even older. Apart from the fact that its lower feathers were matted with balls of mud, its curved backbone was bare, almost as if it had moulted, while the skin on its legs seemed more leathery and wrinkled than before.

'The chase seems to have taken a lot out of it,' observed Sinnéad.

Vickey nodded. 'I'm not surprised. Imagine — man trying to use it like a horse.'

'The poor thing,' said Sinnéad. She was feeling sorry for the big bird, which didn't seem to be as big as it had been the first time they had seen it.

Vickey turned to the pig. 'It wasn't injured, was it?'

The Gaze-pig shook its two heads and whispered back, 'No. It's just tired. You see, it may be a young bird, but it tells me it is growing old.'

The vixens looked at each other and wondered what was happening to the Land of Sinna, the land where the great god Vulpes had said the fox would survive, but where some things were flowering before their time and others were growing old before they had time to be young.

'I think it's time we had another talk with Old Sage Brush,' said Vickey, as they crept back out of the quarry.

Sinnéad nodded. 'So do I.'

~

It was not yet dusk, but the moon had already crept into the sky. It seemed that the wide eye of gloomglow, as the foxes call it, was waiting patiently for darkness to come. The vixens, too, were waiting patiently, and they wondered which would come first, darkness or their mates. Black Tip and Skulking Dog, however, had ranged far and wide in their search for Hop-along, and the valley was already bathed in the half-light of gloomglow by the time they returned.

'Did you find any sign of him?' asked Vickey.

'We tracked him as far as the river,' Black Tip told her.

'But he covered his tracks well,' said Skulking Dog. 'Whatever he's doing, he's made sure we can't follow him.'

'Have you told She-la?' asked Sinnéad.

Skulking Dog nodded. 'She would look for him herself, but she has to stay with the cubs. We told her he would probably turn up during the night.'

'And if he doesn't?' asked Sinnéad.

'We said we'd go out and look for him again,' said Skulking Dog. 'But Hop-along knows what he's doing. He can look after himself.'

'As long as the Fo-paw's not looking for him,' said Vickey. She sighed. 'Anyway, we think it's time we had a long talk with Old Sage Brush.'

'Why?' asked Black Tip. 'What's wrong?'

'It's the Liesalot,' Sinnéad told him. 'There's something very peculiar about it.'

Skulking Dog laughed. 'You can say that again!'

'I don't mean that,' said Sinnéad. 'But since it was chased by man and his dogs, it isn't the same.'

'In what way?' asked Black Tip.

'I know it's hard to believe,' said Sinnéad, 'but it's older somehow.'

'It seems to be ageing very quickly,' explained Vickey. 'I don't know why, but I think we should talk to Old Sage Brush.'

The dog foxes nodded, and the four of them made their way up to the oak tree where the old fox lived.

Old Sage Brush, who had reached the stage where he was very conscious of his own ageing, listened carefully to what the two vixens had to say.

'We're dealing with creatures we don't understand,' said Vickey. 'I mean, I know they came from the big house, but where do they really come from? Where are their parents, and where are their mates?'

'Maybe they have no mates,' suggested Sinnéad.

'But that's not natural,' said Vickey.

'Maybe the Liesalot has been eating the wrong food,' said Black Tip. 'I've seen it eating stones.'

'I've seen hens eating stones,' said Skulking Dog. 'Well, smaller stones, but it didn't seem to do them any harm.'

'All birds eat stones,' Old Sage Brush told them. 'I think it helps their digestion. Anyway, what do you think we should do?'

'I think we should take them back to the big house,' Vickey told him.

'How can we take them back,' asked Skulking Dog, 'when they won't do anything we ask them?'

'We don't have to ask them,' Vickey argued. 'They followed us here, remember? So maybe they would follow us back.'

'But would that not be dangerous?' asked Sinnéad, who had no wish to see the big house again.

'Of course it would be dangerous,' said Black Tip. 'But no more dangerous than having them stay here.'

Skulking Dog turned to his mate. 'They're right, Sinnéad. We've got to get them away from here, and even if it means going back to the big house, I think we should do it.'

'I think,' said Old Sage Brush, 'we'd all feel a lot safer if these creatures were back at the big house. And if there is something wrong with the Liesalot — well, if man has reared it, he might know how to cure it.'

'We must do it before man and his dogs come again,' said Black Tip.

'When would you suggest?' asked the old fox.

Skulking Dog looked at Black Tip, saying, 'They refuse to leave the quarry in the dark, even to graze.'

Black Tip nodded. 'But we could do it before the darkness comes again.'

'At dusk, then,' said the old fox. 'When man has left the fields and the scent has left the grass.' He turned to go back to his earth beneath the tree, adding, 'In the meantime, let's hope the Gaze-pig can keep them out of sight.'

When the moon has taken on the fullness and colour of their own eyes, foxes love to hunt. For the wide eye of gloomglow seems to smile upon them, and gives them enough light to see but not be seen. Rabbits will also come out to feed in the half-light of gloomglow, in the mistaken belief that it will give them the same protection. However, in the absence of man, the moonlit fields become the kingdom of the fox, and the rabbits discover, to their cost, that they cannot see as well as it can, or run as fast. And so, after their discussion with

Old Sage Brush, the other four foxes split up, Black Tip and Vickey going one way, Skulking Dog and Sinnéad another.

The rabbits, the foxes found, were not as reticent about coming out to feed as those on the far side of the valley, and for this they were grateful. Apart from the fact that it made hunting easier, it was a sign that the Fo-paw was still keeping to its own side of the river. If that was so, it would suggest that the attack on Hop-along was an isolated incident. None of them expressed their fears to Old Sage Brush, but, after the attack on Hop-along, they were afraid that the Fo-paw might be intent on seeking out the weaker members of their group. That was why they were spending more time with him than they normally would — something Black Tip and Vickey were able to do without making him suspicious, as they were unable to use their den in the quarry.

As they hunted, the four foxes also kept an eye out for Hop-along. They couldn't imagine where he had gone, but, as there was no further sign of the Fo-paw, they were reasonably hopeful that he was safe. They also wondered about the other creatures that had come from the big house, and, as they looked up occasionally at the wide eye of gloomglow, they couldn't help but wonder if it was all a dream. A bird with two heads! A pig with two faces! And a creature that was neither fox nor cat, but a bit of both! And then there were the others ....

Whatever else they did, they knew they had to get the creatures back to the big house. Otherwise, they would have to abandon the Land of Sinna, and that was something none of them wanted to contemplate.

Having caught rabbits for themselves, the four foxes met up again and made their way back to the wood.

There they gave a rabbit to Old Sage Brush and buried another for him outside between the roots of the oak tree. They had two left, and these they took down to the blackthorns for She-la and the cubs. They told She-la that they still hadn't seen any sign of Hop-along, but reassured her by pointing out that they hadn't seen any sign of the Fo-paw either. In any event, they all knew that Hop-along liked to show he could still hunt for himself, and, for a fox with three legs, that could be a long-drawn-out process.

As they talked, Blaze and Firefly emerged from the earth and tore into one of the rabbits. In a rare display of annoyance, She-la bared her teeth and told them to take it below, while she herself lay down and began nibbling at the other one. She was, her friends could see, preoccupied with thoughts of Hop-along, so they lay down beside her and watched as the wide eye of gloomglow faded and finally gave way to the dawn. Below them, an early-morning mist clung to the sides of the valley, and as they watched it retreat towards the meadows, it thinned to reveal the Liesalot and the Dillylama grazing in a field below the old quarry.

'And there's the Gaze-pig,' said Vickey, getting to her feet. 'I thought he said he was going to try and keep them in the quarry.'

The others were standing up now too, and they could see the pig turning over clods of turf as its two noses sniffed out and dug up roots of one kind or another.

'So he did,' said Black Tip.

Skulking Dog looked around. 'There's still no sign of man. I think we should go down and see if we can get them to keep out of sight until dusk.'

'The mist is lifting,' Sinnéad observed, 'and when it does, they'll be in full view of the whole valley.'

She-la got up. 'I'll go with you. Maybe the Gaze-pig will have news of Hop-along.'

'And what about the cubs?' asked Sinnéad.

She-la looked at the rabbit, which she had barely touched, and said, 'All they're interested in is their stomachs, and they've enough here to keep them occupied.'

Not wishing to be seen themselves, the foxes made their way through the blackthorns, down along the row of beeches at the far end and across by various hedges until they came to where the creatures were grazing.

Calling the Gaze-pig over to them, Black Tip said, 'I thought you said you were going to keep an eye on them.'

The pig snorted through both his noses, to dislodge soil which had lodged in them, and replied, 'I am keeping an eye on them — all three eyes.'

'Gaze-pig,' said Vickey sternly, 'this is no time to be funny. Man will come after them again — and you know what happened to the Liesalot the last time.'

The pig snorted again and smiled. 'I'm not really being funny. I tried to make them stay in the quarry, but they wouldn't. And why should I stay in it on my own? I have two mouths to feed too.'

She-la was about to ask the pig if he had seen Hop-along when there was an ear-piercing screech and a loud 'cock-a-doodle-do' from the direction of the beech trees. Startled, the foxes looked up to see the Cock-a-doodle-sham-cock come floating down from the trees and land a short distance from the Liesalot. It then fanned out its long tail and shivered it in the way that peacocks do, but this time it didn't disappear.

Instead it lowered its tail again and began walking around, every now and then uttering another ear-piercing screech.

The forbidden word was about to explode from Black Tip's lips when, to add to their alarm, the Ewe-ni-horn came racing across the field and skidded to a stop.

'Tell that bird to keep quiet,' Black Tip told the pig. 'And what —' He was about to ask what the Ewe-ni-horn thought it was doing when the animal came running backwards at great speed, brandishing the horn where it should have had a tail, and scattered them in all directions.

The Cock-a-doodle-sham-cock was still uttering the harshest of calls, and when Skulking Dog had jumped out of the way of the Ewe-ni-horn, he asked the pig, 'Can you not keep that bird quiet? You'd think it was deliberately trying to tell man where you and your friends are.'

'It's not trying to tell man where we are,' the pig replied. 'It's trying to tell *us* where *man* is. And the Ewe-ni-horn is trying to get us to move before he comes.'

'You mean man is coming?' asked She-la.

The pig nodded, and Vickey looked around, asking, 'Where? I can't see him.'

'The Liesalot!' exclaimed Sinnéad. 'Ask the Liesalot.'

Hearing her, the Liesalot immediately wrapped its necks around each other and, as usual, pointed its beaks in opposite directions. To add to the confusion, the cubs had arrived on the scene. Oblivious to the danger they were in, they were determined to show that they knew the secret way of getting the Liesalot to tell the lie that would give them the truth.

The big bird had uncurled its necks and was scanning the fields in all directions. Before She-la could stop them, the cubs asked the nearest head, 'Which way does your other head say man is coming?'

The head to which the cubs had spoken looked

towards the wood, saying, 'That way.' Realising that this must be a lie, the foxes were about to take off towards the wood when the same head turned towards the river and said, 'That way.'

The foxes were now about to bolt towards the river, but they were confused, so they held their ground. At the same time, the Dillylama seemed to whisper something to the Liesalot. After some hesitation, the big bird lowered its long necks, as if it was trying to keep out of sight, and walked away quickly towards the old quarry, while the Dillylama took off, twisting and turning like a falling sycamore seed so that it seemed to be going in all directions at the same time.

'What happened, Gaze-pig?' asked Blaze. 'Did we not ask the right question?'

'You asked the right question, all right,' the pig assured her. 'The problem is, man is coming from both directions, and the Dillylama is trying to draw him away from us. Time to go.' With that, the Gaze-pig turned and crashed through the nearest hedge, the Ewe-ni-horn bolted into a clump of gorse, the Cock-a-doodle-sham-cock flew back to the beech trees and the foxes scattered in all directions.

In the hope of trapping the creatures between them, the riders and their dogs had split up and come from opposite directions. It might have seemed to them that the foxes had scattered in panic, but in reality, they all knew where they were going. She-la's concern was not for herself, but for the cubs, and she knew the only chance of saving them was to get them back up to the blackthorns. The survival of Old Sage Brush was uppermost in the minds of the others, and they went in various directions, hoping that this would confuse their pursuers and draw them away from the wood.

However, it was not the foxes but the Dillylama that

the men from the circus were after. This time they had come equipped with two lassos, one to throw over each of its heads. But, because of its very indecisiveness, they soon found that they could not anticipate which way it was going to go.

Having heard what had happened to the Liesalot, the Dillylama realised that its fine feet would not serve it well in the meadows or the bog. For some time, it led its pursuers a merry dance through the fields. Then it headed for the wood.

As for the foxes, their race was run. They could only watch and wait, in the hope that the dance of the Dillylama wouldn't lead the fun dogs to Old Sage Brush.

12

The Flight, the Flower
and the Fo-paw

From his hiding-place on the Hill of Hazels, Hop-along
also watched the dance of the Dillylama and, not for
the first time, wondered why man was so anxious to
bring these creatures back to the big house. Man, he
knew, hunted the fox for its fur and the rabbit for food.
But what good was an animal with two heads, or a bird
with two beaks? Or a sheep with a horn where it
should have had a tail? He had, on occasion, seen a
sheep with two lambs or a cow with two calves, and he
could understand that man would want to keep them.
But a beast with two heads? A pig with two faces? He

couldn't imagine why man would want them.

As he thought about the strange creatures that had come to the Land of Sinna, Hop-along also wondered why man should want to keep a bird which called as harshly as the Cock-a-doodle-sham-cock — especially as it lacked the colours of the rainbow bird — and why he should want such an ungainly bird as the Liesalot. It would hardly be for food, he thought. The Cock-a-doodle-sham-cock seemed to fly where it pleased, and the Liesalot — well, it was too big. Unless it was for their eggs. But who could eat an egg as big as the one he had found in the meadow? Man, he knew, did some strange things, but even he could hardly eat an egg as big as that.

Now Hop-along found himself thinking about Old Sage Brush and some of the things he had said, and he wondered once more how an egg could be put back together again. It seemed impossible, but if the old fox said it could be done, then it could be done. According to the cubs, the Gaze-pig knew the answer, and Hop-along wished he could figure it out. But then, he thought, maybe it wasn't very important. What was important, he told himself, was how to get rid of the Fo-paw.

When he arrived at the hill, Hop-along had searched around until he found an abandoned badger sett that had become part of the rabbit warren. Hoping against hope that the strong smell of the rabbits would hide his scent, he had hidden himself in the dark recesses of the sett. Somehow, he knew, the Fo-paw would become aware of his presence and would come looking for him.

However, darkness had come and gone, and now, as he looked across the valley again, he knew She-la and their friends would be worried about him. For a moment he had a great urge to get up and return to the blackthorns, but he resisted the temptation. There was something he had to do, and he wouldn't return until he had done it.

Settling down again, Hop-along wondered what was happening over in the wood. He had seen the fun dogs following the Dillylama into the trees and man galloping in after them. Now he saw the Gaze-pig emerge from the blackthorns. Running quickly, it crossed the line of beech trees, climbed the hill and followed the riders into the wood.

Old Sage Brush was dozing in his earth beneath the oak tree when he heard the Dillylama hopping through the trees. He listened intently as it came to the clearing beside the oak and, finding itself in familiar surroundings, pranced around and around in a circle of indecision, wondering what it should do. The old fox was in no doubt as to what he should do. Hearing the barking of dogs, he immediately climbed up into the hollow recesses of the tree and waited for the danger to pass.

The circus dogs were now bounding through the wood. Seeing them with both its heads as it turned around and around, the Dillylama took off, running forwards and backwards, sideways and all ways in a desperate effort to escape. But while its two-toed feet were small and light, its two-headed body was heavy. It was, in reality, two llamas in one, and the one heart that served them could not cope with both. Heat and exhaustion soon proved to be as big a burden as its two heads, and, slowly but surely, it began to slow down. The barking got louder and louder, and then, as the Dillylama sank to the ground, the dogs bore down on it with the excitement of howling dogs that had run a fox to ground.

The two heads of the Dillylama were raised as high as its long slender necks would allow, and its large chestnut-brown eyes stared back in panic as its tormentors began to run around it. Its long ears were flattened back against its necks, and now and then it gave a high-pitched moan. Then, in a pitiful act of self-preservation, it curled back its lips to reveal rows of grass-stained teeth, spat its defiance and waited to die.

There was, however, something about the dogs that the Dillylama did not know. They were not howling dogs that hunted the fox and the hare. Nor were they what the foxes called 'fun dogs' — the terriers that hunted the fox and the badger and gave man so much fun. They were, as Hop-along had rightly described them, 'funny dogs' — dogs that had been trained to be funny. And as they gathered around the Dillylama, they did what they had been trained to do. Some, like the poodles, sat up and begged, some did backward somersaults, one of them even chased its tail, while others jumped between the heads of the Dillylama as if they were jumping through a hoop.

Had the foxes seen this strange behaviour, they wouldn't have believed it. Nor would the Gaze-pig. Having seen the Dillylama being chased into the wood, he had followed, and, in the belief that his two-headed friend was in mortal danger, he was bearing down on the dancing dogs with the ferocity of a wild boar.

The riders, who hadn't yet caught up with the dogs, scattered in disarray as the pig rushed between them, and when, a few moments later, the dogs took off in pursuit of the pig, the riders followed. They were unaware that the two-headed llama they wanted so much for their circus was lying nearby, but they knew only too well that a pig with two faces would also be a big attraction.

While a pig can run fast, it can only do so in spurts, and the Gaze-pig now began a game of hide-and-seek with his pursuers. Finding a dense patch of under-growth, he would dash inside and wait until they had passed. Then he would take off again and keep going until he found another hiding-place. The fact that he had two faces and three eyes gave him the advantage of being able to see in three directions at the same time. Nevertheless, he was eventually forced to take to the open fields, and it was there that the circus people decided on a plan to catch him.

The riders had been over these fields before, when they had chased the sheep that had a horn where it should have had a tail. As a result, they knew they were approaching a farm where there were flocks of sheep. Some of the fields, they had noticed, were fenced with wire mesh to keep the sheep in. With luck, the same wire would also keep the pig out. After a brief pause to discuss their strategy, they spread out so that they could manoeuvre the pig in that direction.

As the Gaze-pig raced through the fields, he continued to hide behind every hedge or clump of gorse he could find. He was breathing heavily, and he longed to wallow in the mud to protect his bare back from the heat of the sun. There was no time for such luxuries, however. His pursuers had spread out, with the result that the dogs found him sooner and his stops became shorter.

Then, as he headed for a high, sprawling hawthorn hedge, he found to his dismay that it was cloaked in sheep-wire. Whatever about a pig with one face, there was no way that he, with his two faces, could squeeze through it.

As the Gaze-pig retraced his steps, he saw the dogs closing in on him again. Realising that he was cornered, he turned and ran towards the hedge again. Why he did so, he did not know, for he knew he could not get through the wire. And yet, in some strange way, he wasn't afraid. While a moment before he had been exhausted, a new sensation now gripped his body, and he found himself running faster than he had ever run before. It was as if the vision that had some-times come into one of his minds was taking over and becoming a reality.

The grass, he could see, was flashing past on either side of him, and then, with his middle eye, he saw the hawthorn hedge looming up in front of him. With what seemed the greatest of ease, he found himself sailing over it, and as he landed on the far side, he heard the dogs barking at their inability to either jump the wire or get through it.

Unaware that he carried the genes — and the athletic ability — of the greyhound pig, the Gaze-pig turned and smiled. In one way he knew that he had done something very unusual, but in another way he felt it was in his nature to do what he had done. In other circumstances he might have wondered how he was going to get out of the sheep-field, but not now. It didn't seem to worry him, and he kept going.

Seeing the pig go, the dogs began an even louder chorus of barking, and when the riders arrived, they wondered where their quarry had gone. Had they been there a little earlier, they would have discovered that the little pig with two faces was, like its ancestors, capable of jumping as high as a five-barred gate. And they might have wondered which would have been the biggest attraction in their circus — an ostrich with two beaks, a llama with two heads, or a pig that could run and jump like a greyhound!

As it was, the riders dismissed the Gaze-pig as just a freak with two faces and, turning their horses, went back up to the wood. The Dillylama, however, had gone. In a rare display of decisiveness — brought on, no doubt, by the fear of being hunted — it had waited only until its heart had stopped thumping before getting back on its feet and making a beeline for the quarry. Had the dogs been trained to hunt, they would have followed its scent, but, being performing dogs, they chased only what they could see, and now they could see no sign of any of the creatures. And so the riders returned to the big house once more, to report their failure and frustration to the man in the white coat.

Having seen the riders and dogs pursue the Dillylama into the wood, Hop-along had waited a little longer. Then, when they had failed to emerge, he had hunted for mice and snails and any other food he could find before returning to the badger sett. He had taken quite a risk by going onto the hill like that, but hunger had driven him to it — hunger, and the knowledge that he must leave a fresh scent if the Fo-paw was to find it.

As Hop-along entered the sett, he found the smell of the rabbits very strong, and he hoped it would disguise his scent well enough to conceal his hiding-place. While he wanted the Fo-paw to know he was on the hill, he didn't want it to find him. The rabbits, he knew, were aware of his presence and had retreated to the inner runs of their burrows, where neither foxes nor badgers could follow. He, too, decided to go deeper into the sett, and searched around until he found a hiding-place high up among the roots of the hazels. There he squeezed in as far as he could, and, with his tail tucked up and his nose lying along his front paw, he waited.

Time passed, and the rabbits, forgetting that they had a visitor in the badger sett adjoining their warren, began hopping along the various runs that they considered to be part of their home. Above them, hidden behind the roots of the hazels, Hop-along watched. Now and then a rabbit would go scudding past and he would wonder where it was going in such a hurry. Others would hop past more slowly, one or two even stretching up to sniff at the roots where he lay. Occasionally two of them became embroiled in a fight, squealing and scratching until their fur flew. Then they were gone, and all that remained was pieces of fur.

As Hop-along watched these comings and goings, he sometimes felt a great urge to jump down and seize one of the rabbits. Indeed, he might even have succumbed to the temptation, were it not for the fact that he was wedged so tightly into his hiding-place. Then he reminded himself that it was not part of his plan. Hungry as he was, the last thing he wanted was to be caught eating a rabbit, or to leave the remains of a rabbit that would betray his presence. And so, unaware that one of their greatest predators was looking down at them, the rabbits continued to frisk and frolic along the darkened passages and fight about things that only they understood.

Few other animals would have had the patience to lie and wait for as long as Hop-along had waited, but then, there are few hunters as patient as a fox, especially one with three legs. Except, perhaps, a cat — or an animal that is half-cat, half-fox.

Hop-along found himself dozing and tried not to. He didn't want to make any sound that would tell either the rabbits or the Fo-paw that he was there. In spite of his efforts, however, he felt himself drifting off into sleep, and he thought he heard the voice of

Ratwiddle. It seemed to be coming to him on the wind, and it was saying:

Run, rabbit, run,
The fox will chase,
The cat will pounce,
Two heads in one,
And the tail wags the cat ....

Hop-along woke with a start. Moving only the eye with which he could see the tunnel below him, he wondered what had wakened him. Ratwiddle's voice? Or had that been a dream? A sound, perhaps? With the merest twitch of his ears, which were pinned close to his head by the soil above him, he listened intently.

No, it was not a sound. It was the silence! The rabbits had gone, and he was alone. Or was he? He listened intently again. Still, he could hear nothing.

And then he became aware of another presence, a presence so stealthy it made no sound. A moment later, he saw a dark shadow in the tunnel. It was too big to be a rabbit, and he knew the Fo-paw had come looking for him.

Even though Hop-along had been expecting the Fo-paw to come, his heart sank. What if it saw a beam of daylight glinting in his eye? He closed his eyes and listened. He could hear it breathing as it sniffed around, and he tried not to breathe himself in case it heard him. It was coming closer, and, while he couldn't see it, he knew it was sniffing the air and then the ground as it moved. Strong though the scent of the rabbits was, he knew it had also detected the scent of fox.

Now, for the first time, Hop-along felt the urge to run. But where? Had he taken the advice that Old Sage Brush was so fond of giving, he would have hidden himself near one of the escape routes badgers always had at the rear of their setts. And he would have bolted. But would he have made it? Hardly. Not a fox with three legs.

The thought settled him for a moment, and he kept perfectly still. The Fo-paw, he could tell, was dangerously close, and he could imagine its tail flicking from side to side as it tried to figure things out. Then he heard it snort, probably to blow away a piece of the rabbit-fur that had settled on the floor of the tunnel. This seemed to distort its sense of smell, maybe even upset its concentration, and he heard it turn. Cautiously he opened his eye and, to his great relief, saw that it had gone.

Hardly daring to breathe again, Hop-along continued to watch and wait. Combining as it did the qualities of the cat and the fox, the Fo-paw was, he knew, a very skilful hunter. Perhaps it was hiding in a side-tunnel, waiting for him to make the next move. If that was so, then he would make sure the next move was not his.

After a while, Hop-along tried to ease the cramps that were creeping into his bones, but he couldn't move, so he closed his eyes again and did what he did best. He waited and waited, and then, just when he thought he could wait no longer, a rabbit hopped out of the warren and into the sett beside him. It was followed by another, then another. Hop-along knew by the way the rabbits were moving that they were going to the entrance to await the arrival of dusk. Their movements also told him that the way was clear for him too, and, with not a little difficulty, he extricated himself from his hiding-place. The rabbits ahead of him immediately dashed out and around to another entrance, while those behind bolted back the way they had come. All, that is, except one. It couldn't make up its mind which way to go, and Hop-along's hungry wait was rewarded at last. He smiled to himself. Rabbits, he thought, had their dillies too!

By the time Hop-along had satisfied his hunger, the aches and pains he had suffered in his cramped hiding-place had almost disappeared, and he hobbled towards the entrance of the sett. There he found that the day had lost its warmth but dusk had not yet come. Some distance out, he picked up the scent of the Fo-paw. Now he knew the direction it had taken when it had left the warren.

While Old Sage Brush would have described Hop-along's plan as one worthy of his species, he would also have considered it foolhardy in the extreme, especially for a fox with only three legs. For he proceeded to follow the Fo-paw's scent down through the fields. Having risked death by luring the creature up to the warren, he was intent on tracking it back to its den.

Hop-along, of course, was acutely aware of the danger that might await him at every turn, but he kept going. The scent led him down to the meadows, and soon he found himself looking at the clump of giant weeds at the bend in the river. The magpie was back, perched precariously on the topmost branches, its long tail flicking as it tried to keep its balance. Suddenly Hop-along began to think about tails again — the long tails of the long-tailed tits, the flicking tails of the wagtails, and now the flicking tail of the magpie. The magpie uttered a harsh chatter, and he was afraid it might draw the attention of the Fo-paw to him. He stopped and looked around. The meadow was clear. He kept going, and as he drew closer, the magpie gave another squawk and flew off.

The pungent smells of man's rubbish and of the clump of giant weeds superseded the scent of the Fo-paw, and Hop-along couldn't tell whether it had gone inside the clump or bypassed it. Unable to proceed with any degree of certainty, he retraced his steps and, from what he considered to be a safe distance, lay down to consider his next step.

A gentle breeze was still blowing across the meadows, and as he pondered his predicament, he heard once again the voice of the great god Vulpes, saying:

> *Listen to the wind. Listen to the wind, for it caresses*
> *Mother Earth and tells you all you need to hear ....*
> *Caress the wind. Caress the wind, for it listens to*
> *Mother Earth and shows you all you need to see ....*

Closing his eyes, Hop-along raised his head into the evening breeze. He felt it caress his nose and stroke his ears, and it told him all he needed to hear and showed him all he needed to see. The Fo-paw had gone to the river to drink, and when it returned to its den, he would be waiting for it.

At the entrance to the clump of weeds, he noticed the crumpled remains of a huge black-and-yellow-striped caterpillar and wondered if the magpie had been complaining about that or about him. Probably both, he thought. He also wondered why the caterpillar, like the weeds, had grown so big. Its odour was anything but appetising, so he sidestepped it and cautiously ventured inside.

Down at the river, the Fo-paw heard the magpie chattering and looked up to see it flying away. The creature knew immediately that it had a visitor. It also knew that the sun had not set and that it was too early for the rabbits.

Once inside the clump of weeds, Hop-along could see that a well-worn path ran through it. The path had been trodden by cattle or sheep, or perhaps even by man, and it separated to go around each side of a group of giant stems that grew in the middle. Beyond these stems, close to the exit on the far side, was the giant daisy that he had seen devouring a rabbit. Taking care to keep well clear of it, he nosed around and, close by, located a patch of flattened grass. This, he reckoned, was the den of the Fo-paw. With the smell of the rubbish and the weeds, he couldn't detect the creature's scent, and he grudgingly conceded that it had chosen well. He then retreated to the other side of the weeds that grew in the middle, concealed himself in the long grass and waited.

This time, Hop-along didn't have to wait long. He had hardly settled himself when he saw the Fo-paw framed in the light of the entrance, beside the giant daisy.

It paused for a moment, to allow its eyes to adjust to the gloomy interior, and looked around. Its ears, the short ears of a cat, twitched as it tried to pinpoint the location of the intruder it knew was there. At the same time its nose, the long nose of a fox, sniffed for the scent, but the tangle of other smells that had cloaked its own scent also cloaked the scent of the intruder. And all the while its tail, the long, sloping tail of a cat, flicked from side to side.

From his hiding-place, Hop-along caught glimpses of the Fo-paw as it moved in on the other side of the central group of weeds. It bypassed the rabbit-eating daisy, sniffed to see if anything had been in its den and then lay down in it. He knew it was laying claim to its den, and, while it might have looked as if it had settled itself, he could see that its eyes were scanning every nook and cranny of its lair.

A moment later, their eyes met, and they rose up — the Fo-paw to catch an enemy that was weak, Hop-along to confront an adversary that was strong.

The Fo-paw bared its teeth and stepped forward, the end of its tail flicking from side to side as it contemplated a quick kill. But as it dashed one way, Hop-along hopped the other. When the Fo-paw changed direction, Hop-along did likewise, and so the deadly game of cat-and-mouse went on. However, Hop-along was no mouse. With each hop he took, he made sure the weeds that grew in the middle of the clump were between him and the Fo-paw. Furthermore, his moves were not entirely in response to those of the Fo-paw. All the time he was trying to manoeuvre it into a certain position.

As Hop-along continued to stay out of the clutches of the Fo-paw, he could see that it was getting more and more annoyed and that its tail was flicking in an ever-widening sweep. The Fo-paw moved again, and so did he. A little bit more, he told himself. A little bit more. It was almost in position ....

Now, he thought. That should do it.

The Fo-paw flicked its tail again, and this time it came to rest on one of the large leaves of the giant daisy. The sticky globules held it fast, and it turned, like a cat, to claw at the plant, only to find that it had put its paw into a glue-like secretion that wouldn't let go. Instinctively it clawed at the leaf with its other paw, and, as it hissed and spat, Hop-along could see that its reaction was not that of a fox, but of a cat.

Soon its body was also caught up in the glue, and as it continued to struggle, its other enemy, the fox that had dared to enter its den, was forgotten.

Hop-along hobbled out into the meadow and, with a last look back at the clump of weeds that had caused him so much trouble, headed back across the river. Half a fox, he reckoned, was no match for a whole fox — even one with three legs!

13

The Wind of Change

The Gaze-pig lay outside the blackthorns and, with his two faces and three eyes, could see all there was to see. With the eye on one of his faces, he had seen Black Tip and Vickey, Skulking Dog and Sinnéad emerging from the wood and crossing over into the old quarry. With the eye on his other face, he was watching She-la, who was sitting outside her earth waiting anxiously for any sign of Hop-along while at the same time keeping an eye on the two young foxes who were playing near their earth.

With his third eye, the one between his two faces, the Gaze-pig had watched the sun turn red and sink towards the Hill of Hazels. As it began to disappear, a movement at the quarry caught his attention, and he saw the four foxes slipping back out, but instead of returning to the wood, they went down through the fields to the meadows. A short time later, the Liesalot emerged from the quarry, followed by the Dillylama and the Ewe-ni-horn. Nibbling at the grass as they went, they slowly made their way down after the foxes.

A harsh shriek, followed by a loud 'cock-a-doodle-do', told the foxes in the meadow that their plan was working. The Cock-a-doodle-sham-cock, which was perching on a small ash tree not far from the quarry, had no intention of being left on its own. Having uttered its now-familiar call, it broke into flight and sailed down after its friends.

The foxes were anxious that the creatures should follow them across the river, so they made sure that they didn't get too far ahead. They also chose a shallow part of the river to cross, as they didn't want the Ewe-ni-horn to be left behind, and they were relieved when all three creatures followed. As for the Cock-a-doodle-sham-cock, it flew ahead and waited on the clump of giant weeds at the bend in the river.

To their surprise, the foxes met Hop-along on the far side of the river and wondered why, in view of the fact that the Fo-paw seemed determined to get him, he had decided to go back there. However, he just smiled and told them they needn't worry about him, or about the Fo-paw. It had, he said, met its match.

Before they could ask him any more, they heard the Cock-a-doodle-sham-cock screeching again, and, looking up, they saw the man in the white coat emerging from the clump of weeds. He was carrying something, and Hop-along wondered if he had succeeded in extricating the Fo-paw from the giant daisy. One way or the other, he knew it would bother him no more, so he headed back towards the blackthorns.

It was the Gaze-pig who first spotted Hop-along. By this time, She-la had begun to fear the worst, and when he drew her attention to the fact that her mate was coming, she could hardly believe her eyes. She immediately instructed the young foxes to stay where they were, and raced down to the meadows to meet him.

If She-la was surprised to see Hop-along returning to the blackthorns, the man in the white coat was amazed to see most of his creations going back across the valley. He had come down to burn the weeds, and he was appalled to see how fast they were growing. The giant caterpillar, he reckoned, was a product of the same process, but the toxins in the superweeds had obviously been too strong even for it. Looking up, he saw, to his consternation, that the seed-heads of the giant spear thistle had ripened rapidly. With a furtive glance around to make sure he wasn't being observed, he bent down and made his way inside. There he found that the Fo-paw had fallen foul of the sundew. He immediately threw some inflammable liquid onto the sundew, pulled the Fo-paw clear and carried it outside. He was about to set fire to the weeds when he heard a screech and saw the Cock-a-doodle-sham-cock sailing away towards the Hill of Hazels.

Afraid that, if he set fire to the weeds, he might frighten his other creatures away, the man in the white coat made his way back up towards the big house. The Fo-paw, he could see, was in a bad way, and he feared it might not survive the cleaning that would be needed to remove the digestive juices of the sundew from its fur. In any event, it would have to wait. Back in his laboratory, he put it into one of his cages. Then, taking the buckets with which he used to feed the other creatures, he hurried back down the fields.

The light was fading fast, and it seemed that the Liesalot and its friends had decided to stop in the meadows, when the foxes heard man calling from the direction of the big house. He was also waving his buckets, and they wondered what he was doing.

The other creatures, of course, knew immediately what he was doing. He was letting them know that he was going to feed them.

Without a moment's hesitation, the Liesalot and the Ewe-ni-horn set off at a gallop towards him. The Dillylama, unsure as always as to what it should do, pranced around a time or two, then followed. By the time they got to the man in the white coat, the Cock-a-doodle-sham-cock was already there, and, like the animals that took refuge in the ark, all four of them followed him back up to the enclosure behind the big house.

The Liesalot, the man could see, had grown old as prematurely and as quickly as the superweeds, while the Dillylama seemed to be very tired. The Ewe-ni-horn was as sprightly as ever and the Cock-a-doodle-sham-cock was still in fine voice, but he would have to examine them, too, for any signs of premature ageing. There was no sign of the Gaze-pig, but it had been cloned from a pig that was a slow grower, and it might not develop the same problem. With a little luck, it might also be tempted to come back. As he filled their buckets with food, the man knew he would have to keep his creations under observation for a while longer, especially the Liesalot and the Dillylama. The circus people wouldn't be happy, but then, if the creatures aged and died prematurely, they wouldn't be happy with that either.

Darkness had fallen by the time the man in the

white coat returned to the big house. The Fo-paw, he could see, was still unconscious. For a long time he worked to remove the secretion of the sundew from its fur. Then he dried it and wrapped it in a warm blanket.

He had been taken aback by the sheer size and strength of the sundew, and by the discovery that it and the other weeds had resisted the strongest weed-killer he could devise. If they went to seed and spread, they would, he knew, cause an ecological disaster. It was imperative, therefore, that they should be destroyed as soon as possible.

The sun had not yet returned to the sky, but the dawn it would bring was already beginning to lift the darkness from the Land of Sinna. Up in the wood, the Gaze-pig trotted through the trees between the two young foxes. As usual, they were plying him with all sorts of questions, some of which he would answer and some of which he would not. He told them, for example, that it was not his intention to return to the big house, as he was enjoying his freedom too much. However, when they asked him if he had really run like the wind or if he had really jumped a high hedge, he merely shrugged his hairy shoulders and said, 'Now, what do you think?'

Some of their other questions he would also answer with more questions, and as they tried to come up with the right answers, he would watch them with the eye on the side of each face, while using the middle eye to see where he was going.

'You said you knew the answer to Old Sage Brush's question,' said Blaze.

'Which question was that?' the Gaze-pig asked.

'You know,' said Firefly, 'the one about the egg.'

The Gaze-pig smiled. 'I never knew he asked such a question.'

'Well,' said Blaze, 'I suppose he didn't really ask the question. But he said there was a creature that could put a broken egg back together again, and the question has been in all our minds since. Which creature is it?'

'I mean,' added Firefly, 'it's difficult to imagine that any creature could put an egg back together again, even if it wanted to.'

The Gaze-pig stopped and smiled at them with both of his faces. 'There's only one creature that can put an egg together,' he told them, 'and that's a bird.'

'We know that,' said Blaze. 'But if the egg gets broken, which creature can put it back together again?'

The Gaze-pig shook both its faces. 'The answer's still the same.' Seeing that they still didn't understand, he explained, 'If you break an egg and swallow it, that's the end of it. But what happens if a bird has absolutely nothing left in its stomach and eats the broken egg?'

Blaze smiled triumphantly. 'It'll lay it again!'

'That's right,' Firefly exclaimed. 'It'll put it back together again. Wait until we tell Old Sage Brush!'

'Well, don't tell him I told you,' said the Gaze-pig. He smiled until his hairy shoulders shook and added, 'I wouldn't want him to think I was two-faced!'

When they arrived at the oak tree, the young foxes found, to their disappointment, that Old Sage Brush was not in his earth. The scents told them that he had left with Sinnéad and Skulking Dog, but where he had gone, they couldn't imagine. So they lay down in the long grass with the Gaze-pig, to await his return.

~

During the night, Black Tip and Vickey had gone out to hunt, and instead of going back to the oak tree, they had returned to their own den in the old quarry. The scent of the Liesalot and its friends was still very strong, and some of the bushes in the quarry had been nibbled bare. Nevertheless, Black Tip and his mate were happy to be back, and just before daylight they went up to the rim of the quarry to watch the wide eye of gloomglow fade into the dawn.

Skulking Dog and Sinnéad had also gone out to hunt, and, for the first time in a long while, they had taken Old Sage Brush with them. He himself, of course, was not able to hunt, but he lay and waited for them. He caressed the wind with his nose and listened to what it had to say, and it told him what they were doing. Then, carrying a rabbit apiece, they went down to the blackthorns to see Hop-along. Like everyone else, the old fox was eager to hear how Hop-along had got the better of the Fo-paw, and what better way to hear the story than over a good meal?

As the light of day spread across the valley, so too did another light — one that was man-made. Alerted by Black Tip and Vickey, the others came out of the blackthorns and, in ones and twos, made their way along the valley to a field overlooking the bend in the river. There, they told Old Sage Brush, the man in the white coat had set fire to the clump of giant weeds.

A cloud of thick smoke now drifted down the valley, and whether man saw it or not, the foxes could not tell, but a huge star of thistledown drifted down with it. A moment later another followed, then another, as the giant spear thistle released its seed before the fire could consume it.

The foxes turned to go. As far as they were concerned, the valley had returned to normal. They were unaware that one man, at least, had gone too far. He had, as the old fox had feared, broken the laws of nature, and things would never be the same again.

Author's Note

While the effects of genetic engineering described in this story are obviously exaggerated, they are, I believe, a reflection of the fears many people have about what could happen as experiments continue with cloning and genetically modified food. These fears may well be unfounded, and some of the developments could turn out to be of benefit to mankind — for example, the cloning of parts for the human body. Nevertheless, such fears do exist. Britain's Minister for Consumer Affairs, Kim Howells, was reported in *The Sunday Times* on 6 June 1999 as saying that he was choosing not to eat genetically modified food because, by consuming it, 'you could end up with three heads'. He was jesting, of course, but he revealed that, to avoid any risk, he grew all his own vegetables on an allotment at his home.

The scientist and the clones that feature in this story are, needless to say, figments of my imagination. The idea for the Gaze-pig came from images of two pigs which I came across while thinking of the characters I would use. One was a two-headed pig called Rudy, which, according to a photo-report in *The Irish Times* on 14 April 1998, was sold to a Los-Angeles-based animal rescue centre. Most two-headed pigs, the report said, are stillborn or die shortly after birth, but Rudy was nearly a year old when the photograph was taken. The other was a greyhound pig, a likeness of which I saw in the Ulster Folk and Transport Museum, Cultra, Holywood, Co. Down. It seems to have been a small, hairy-backed pig, with upward-pointing tusks and two fleshy appendages, called wattles, hanging from its throat. An explanatory notice in the museum says that greyhound pigs were common in the eighteenth and early nineteenth centuries. Apart from their long snouts and wattles, they were also remarkable for their agility. It was claimed that a greyhound pig could easily jump over a five-barred gate. They were slow-growing, but were valued for the quality of their meat and as foundation stock for cross-breeding. They survived into this century, but in very small numbers. The last recorded sighting of them, the museum says, was in Liverpool, where it was claimed that during the Second World War an Irish man kept some foraging on a city rubbish dump.

My reference in Chapter 10 to the ostrich as a bird that is lacking in wisdom, and to the grasshopper, comes from the Book of Job, Chapter 39, which reads:

> She is hardened against her young ones, as though they were not hers .... Because God hath deprived her of wisdom, neither hath he imparted to her understanding .... She scorneth the horse and his rider. Hast thou given the horse strength? Canst thou make him afraid as the grasshopper?

Acknowledgements

I must thank Brendan McWilliams for his observations on the wind in his Weather Eye column in *The Irish Times*. In this column, he also referred to the poem 'Address to a Child, during a Boisterous Winter Evening' by William Wordsworth, part of which I have quoted in Chapter 1 — 'Which way does the wind come? Which way does he go?...' My thanks also to my daughters, Samantha and Simone, for helping me source other poems by Wordsworth and material on cloning; Dr William Reville, senior lecturer in biochemistry at University College Cork, for telling us, in his column in *The Irish Times*, how to unscramble eggs; Dr John O'Donoghue, for his saying, 'To the fearful eye, all is threatening,' in *Anam Cara: Spiritual Wisdom from the Celtic World*; our dear friend, the late Nuala McGlynn, for introducing me to that book; Lisa Maybury, for her observations on her pet rabbit; and my wife Frances and my family, for their continuing support. Also, a special word of thanks to my editor at Wolfhound Press, Eilís French, for the detailed and sensitive manner in which she edited my manuscript.

Tom McCaughren
1999

Also by Tom McCaughren

Run with the Wind

A fox legend says that, even if foxes are driven out of the
rest of the country, they will survive in the beautiful valley
which they call the Land of Sinna.

But now fur companies have turned to the Land of Sinna for
supplies, and the foxes are being hunted almost to extinction.
Vickey, Black Tip, Fang and wise Old Sage Brush
set out on a quest for the secret of survival,
which they know lies somewhere within the valley.

'Entertainment and suspense at its best,
it is the *Watership Down* of the fox world.'
The Irish Times

ISBN 0-86327-568-0

Run to Earth

It is cubbing time, and the foxes — Vickey and Black Tip,
Sinnéad and Skulking Dog, She-la and Hop-along —
are looking forward to the arrival of their cubs.
But their fight for survival must go on.
The moons of death strike in the dead of night. Even the
blue skies of the day are dark with danger. And the greatest
threat of all comes from the foxes' oldest enemy — man.

Desperate to protect their cubs, the foxes are forced
to run to earth. But even their earths are no longer safe ....

'The book is irresistible.'
Books Ireland

ISBN 0-86327-569-9

Also by Tom McCaughren

Run Swift, Run Free

It is summer in the Land of Sinna — time for
Young Black Tip, Little Running Fox, Twinkle, Scat and Scab
to learn to fend for themselves.

How many of these daring cubs will live to the end of summer?
Have they learned from wise Old Sage Brush
the secrets and skills they need in order to survive?

'Wonderfully observed from Nature ...
set to become a classic of universal appeal.'
RTÉ Guide

ISBN 0-86327-593-1

Run to the Ark

When Twinkle discovers a valley of dead foxes and badgers,
the foxes and their friends begin a great journey.
They are searching for a safe home, the place at the very Edge
of the World — the place foretold by the Bow in the Cloud.

But both man and their natural enemies are waiting for them,
ready to engage them in a fight to the death.

'You could almost believe that Tom McCaughren has
some magical way of making himself small and invisible
so that he can live among the foxes, badgers and otters
whose lives he describes so well.'
The Irish Times

ISBN 0-86327-594-X

Also by Tom McCaughren

Run to the Wild Wood

'And death shall never find us in the bosom of the fragrant wood ....'

But the old saying hasn't come true for the badgers.
The Fragrant Wood which sheltered them
for hundreds of years is gone, destroyed by man.
In desperation, they turn to the foxes for help.

Wise Old Sage Brush calls on the strength of Fang,
the surefootedness of Hop-along, the loyalty of She-la,
and the youth and speed of Little Running Fox,
Scat, Twinkle and Young Black Tip;
and together they set out on their quest
to lead the badgers to a new home.

But their strange friend Ratwiddle has seen mysterious
and frightening visions of dragons spitting fire
and man running to the earth.
What dangers lie in wait for the foxes and the badgers
as they journey in search of the Valley of the Dragon?

'This beautifully told story is written
with a true sense of the foxes and their lives ....
A truly lovely story for all readers.'
The Examiner

ISBN 0-86327-571-0